# the Passage

Becoming Beka Book 3

# the Passage

Sarah
Anne
Sumpolec

MOODY PUBLISHERS
CHICAGO

© 2005 by
SARAH ANNE SUMPOLEC

ISBN: 0-8024-6453-X
EAN/ISBN-13: 978-0-8024-6453-8


Library of Congress Cataloging-in-Publication Data

Sumpolec, Sarah Anne.
    The passage / Sarah Sumpolec.
        p. cm. — (Becoming Beka ; no. 3)
    Summary: As sixteen-year-old Beka struggles with her feelings about Josh, who is going away to college soon, and Mark, who wants a more physical relationship, Gretchen's threats take a terrifying turn and God does not seem to be paying attention.
    ISBN 0-8024-6453-X
    [1. Dating (Social customs)—Fiction. 2. High schools—Fiction.
3. Schools—Fiction. 4. Fathers and daughters—Fiction. 5. Christian life—Fiction.] I. Title.

PZ7.S9563Pas 2005
[Fic]—dc22

                                                        2004018140


1 3 5 7 9 10 8 6 4 2

*Printed in the United States of America*

*For my Lydia.*
*You are a joy and a treasure.*

# ACKNOWLEDGMENTS

**First, I** want to thank all of the readers who have grown to love Beka. I appreciate all of you, and I look forward to continuing this journey with you. Thanks also go to my husband, Jeff, my very best friend for all day, who has been so supportive. I couldn't have done any of this without your love and encouragement (not to mention your great title suggestions). My three little girls, who let Mommy work on the computer occasionally —you all are wonderful, thank you.

Then there are people who specifically helped in the birth of this particular book. I want to thank Amy Hobart, who helped make sure my paramedics were doing things right and the Spotsylvania Juvenile Court people who helped the fates of certain characters be decided. Thanks to my new editor at Moody, Andy McGuire, who has been great to work with, and to Cheryl Dunlop, who has helped me with her editing prowess since Book 1. A very special thanks to Barb Fisher and her team for the cover design.

But most of all, I am so thankful that God found me when I was lost. It is an honor and a privilege to belong to Him, and were it not for Christ's sacrifice and great love for me, none of this would be possible. Thank You.

Whoa there boy."

I hadn't been in the saddle for two minutes, and the enormous palomino had already squashed my right leg against the wood fence around the paddock. "Ow. C'mon now, move over." I lifted the reins in the direction I wanted him to go, but instead of moving forward, he shifted his weight as if he were actually trying to break my leg.

I looked over where Gabby had finished helping my sister Anna mount Wind Dancer, the little paint horse she had just gotten for her ninth birthday. I didn't want to act like I couldn't handle myself, but my leg was throbbing. I fought with myself for only a moment. Pain was more important than pride.

"Gabby?" I called. She looked at me, and I swear she suppressed a grin, but she ran right over and grabbed the bridle. Asking her, the woman who had been hanging around my father for months, made my throat tighten. I didn't even want her near me.

"What are you doing, you big oaf?" She pulled the bridle, moving the horse forward, instantly allowing the blood flow to return to my leg and making it tingle and itch. "Thunder can be a little headstrong sometimes." She smiled at me.

I didn't smile back. "Then what am I doing on him? Don't you have some nice old horse that can barely walk or something?"

"Thunder'll be fine once we get him out on the trail. We're just too close to his supper." She paused and looked up at me. I felt like I was looming over her, the black helmet on my head adding at least two inches to my height, not to mention being up on the horse.

"You going to be okay? Your dad said you've done this before." She actually sounded a little concerned, which made me want to conquer the big beast before giving her the satisfaction of helping any more.

"I'll be fine." I smiled this time. Well, I tried to smile. She turned and headed back toward Lucy, who was trying to throw a saddle onto the back of a midnight black gelding.

*     *     *

Anna walked Wind Dancer over to where Thunder had found a nice patch of grass to munch on. He seemed to not care in the least that I was on his back.

"Isn't Dancer amazing?" she asked me for about the tenth time that afternoon.

"Yes, amazing," I told her again. "I still can't believe Dad bought you that thing."

"Me neither. I mean, he just had to buy the horse though since Gabby lets him stay here for free. Isn't she awesome?"

*Awesome* wasn't the word that came to mind, so I ignored the question. "You're not going to mind her using him for lessons? Other people riding him?"

"Nope. Because he's my horse. It doesn't matter who rides him 'cause he's still mine. I'm going to warm him up."

She barely moved, but the horse turned easily for her as she clucked her tongue and then walked toward the riding ring. She looked like she was born on the horse, even though she had been riding for only a few months. She had told us that she chose the name Wind Dancer because riding him made her feel like she was dancing with the wind. I envied her.

I shifted my attention back to Gabby as she adjusted Lucy's stirrups. Lucy stretched her leg forward while Gabby buckled the strap and then placed her foot in the stirrup. Gabby pulled on it, slid her hand under the horse's belly, and then gave the black gelding a slap on the rump.

"You're all done. You can go walk him around the ring until we're ready to go," I heard her say.

Lucy pulled back on the left rein and turned her horse toward the ring where Anna was already trotting. I watched her, still getting used to the auburn hair that curled itself up and around the edges of her helmet. She had gone into town with Gabby the night before and come back with a full ten inches chopped off her hair. Apparently, they had found a salon in the mall that was doing a Locks of Love program, where people donate hair to make wigs for sick kids. She decided then and there to get her hair cut. With the heaviness gone, her hair curled softly around the edges. It now fell just below her chin, instead of all the way down her back. She looked so different. And so much more grown up. She would be fourteen in August, but people would probably think she was my age or older.

Maybe I should do something with my hair too. Something drastic. I reached back to touch my own auburn hair that was bundled into a ponytail at the nape of my neck. It was so plain, just long and straight. And boring. Maybe my hair would curl too.

\*       \*       \*

"Hey Beka, you can walk Thunder around the ring for a few minutes. We're almost ready to go," Gabby called as she headed into the barn to get her own horse. My dad had said a family trail ride would be fun, only I didn't think he should have called it a "family" anything. My brother, Paul, *wasn't* there since he was at baseball practice and Gabby was there, and she wasn't part of our family.

I had gotten up that morning determined to try and be nice to Gabby, but I just couldn't do it. I had even tried praying, but it didn't seem to help. My father had promised me that they were just friends and that he still missed my mother too much to even think about anyone else, but I wasn't sure I believed him. He seemed to really enjoy being around her. Anna and Lucy adored her, and then there was me, the only holdout. Mom had only died just over a year ago, and the memories were still raw in my heart. I couldn't even think about a stepmother. The thought made me nauseous. But Gabby spent way too much time with my family for me to be completely naive about what might be going on. My dad and she weren't dating, but I was sure she wanted to.

She had never been married, and it was obvious when she looked at my dad that she cared about him. Too much, in my opinion. I would think that she was after his money, which as a banker he had quite a bit of, but she had plenty of money of her own. She had inherited the horse farm from her grandparents when they died, and now she ran it, giving lessons, boarding horses, and hosting riding shows. But that was part of the problem. When I looked at her, she just always seemed "horse-y," as if she'd just walked off the farm. She was usually in jeans, and her long hair was usually kind of messy. One time she had even tied it back with some twine she pulled off the hay bales. I mean, really. Was that the kind of stepmother I wanted?

I didn't want any stepmother, but she struck me as particularly distasteful. My mother had been a pediatrician, and she always looked stylish even in her white lab coat. She wore dresses and skirts that made her look like a knockout, and now my dad was hanging out with the horsewoman of Bragg County.

*       *       *

"Hey Beka, are you coming with us?" Dad called from the ring, where they had all lined up behind Gabby. Lucy and Anna had been on trail rides before with Gabby and my dad. Up until today, I had always had a reason to get out of it. Until today. It was the first day of spring break, and I couldn't come up with one excuse when they talked about it the night before.

"I'm coming," I called. The line of horses began to move across the clearing toward the woods. "C'mon Thunder," I said as I pulled on the reins. He lifted his head in protest and then returned to the grass he was still eating, pulling me forward in the saddle as he did so. I pulled again and gave him a kick, like Gabby had showed me. He still didn't move. Maybe I didn't kick hard enough. I tried again and this time he lurched forward and headed straight toward Lucy's horse at the back of the line.

I was practically lying on his mane so I tried to return myself to an upright position before I reached everybody. Thunder wasn't trotting, but he was walking fast, and I felt like I was going to slide off one side or the other. I tried to remember the twenty million things Gabby had told me to remember when she had helped me saddle the horse. I really had ridden before, but it had been at a Girl Scout camp where they put all the beginners on these decrepit old horses that couldn't lurch any-where if they tried.

My heart was pounding in my chest, but as soon as Thunder reached the back of the line, he slowed down and simply followed Lucy's horse. By the time we walked onto the trail, I started to relax. Thunder had probably done this a hundred times before, and everything would be fine.

Since we were single file, no one could really talk to each other. Lucy and I could have talked, but she didn't turn around, and I didn't want to start the conversation. I figured she was probably mad at me, because when she came home all excited about her new haircut I hadn't said anything, not because of her but because I felt like Gabby had entirely too much influence over her. Lucy wouldn't have even been at the mall if Gabby hadn't taken her. Lucy had seemed irritated with me ever since then, and I didn't feel like having the argument that was brewing.

So I concentrated on the scenery. At least I did until I got whacked in the face with a branch that swung back at me when Lucy let it go. She called "Branch!" just as it stung my cheek. I knew my cheek was red, because when I touched the skin it felt like it was on fire. After that I concentrated on ducking and twisting to avoid any more renegade branches.

We walked for a long time. I didn't wear a watch, so I wasn't sure how long we had been riding, but I was get-ting bored and my bottom was sore from the saddle. And I was tired of the branches. I was positive I was going to find my face full of red scratches when I got home.

I tried thinking about what kind of dresses I would buy for the two dances I had been invited to. Two dances. Two guys. I shook my head in disbelief. I was pretty sure my dad would be okay with Josh and his homeschool formal, but I wasn't sure about Mark and the junior prom. My brother, Paul, had heard that Mark had a questionable reputation, and even though Mark had confessed his secret to me, I had a feeling it wouldn't ease my brother or father's mind. And then there was Mark and Josh themselves. I had already fallen for Mark. Even with his past, I couldn't help but get all flushed and tongue-tied when he was around and when he looked at me with that adoring look. Besides, I knew how Mark felt about me, or at least what he said he felt, but Josh was still a mystery. A rather intriguing, handsome mystery. One that I kind of wanted to solve.

Finally I saw a break in the trees coming up, and sure enough, we emerged onto another pasture facing the barn, but on the opposite side. I was so relieved that we were done that it caught me off guard when Thunder lurched again. Since he was doing his own thing on the trail, I had let go of the reins, holding onto his mane instead. I gathered the reins back up and pulled up and back on them. He didn't like that and gave a loud whinny, which made everyone turn around to see what I was doing to the horse.

"Make sure he doesn't take off on you," Gabby said as Thunder pulled at the reins by throwing his head side to side, still whinnying.

I was getting scared, and I was actually happy to see Gabby turn around and start riding toward me. I wanted to get off that horse as quickly as possible. I could feel his muscles tense underneath my calves, and he was jumping a little bit as he protested.

Then Anna said something about a bunny, and Thunder reared back on his hind legs, leaving me clutching the saddle to stay on top. Then as soon as his front legs hit the ground, he took off at a full gallop. I felt like a rag doll trying to hold on as I got tossed around on top. I abandoned the reins, grabbing two big chunks of his mane and pulling myself down over the top of the saddle. My teeth felt like they were going to bounce right out of my head, which made me think about what I would look like with dentures. Then Thunder suddenly stopped dead in his tracks.

Only I didn't.

It was impossible to hold on as I felt my body sail into the air. It seemed so slow. I saw his ears, his long pale nose, the ground, and then blue sky. I heard a nicker that sounded as if he was laughing at me. And all I could see was sky. A bright blue sky with perfect cotton clouds. Birds flying overhead and ringing bells . . .

## "Beka! Beka!"

I kept hearing voices, but I couldn't tell where they were coming from.

"Beka! Wake up!"

*What? Why are you yelling?* I lifted my hand to my head. It was throbbing. I tried opening my eyes, but they didn't seem to want to open. It made me tired to try. I just wanted to go back to sleep. Why wouldn't they leave me alone?

"Beka!"

Maybe if I ignored them they'd leave me alone.

"Go call 911, Lucy. Now."

That woke me up. "What? What's wrong?"

"Wait, Lucy. She's waking up."

I moved to sit up but couldn't, so I forced my eyes open. My dad's face was inches away.

"Don't try to sit up yet. Are you okay?"

"Huh? What happened?" When he sat back a bit, I saw the sky again and groaned. That stupid horse threw me. Gabby's face appeared, and I could see Anna clutching at Lucy above my feet.

"Should I go call for help?" Lucy asked.

"No," Gabby said. "I think she just got the wind knocked out of her."

"Are you sure?" Dad said. "She should get checked out, shouldn't she?"

"Let's see how she does. Beka? Does anything hurt?"

I focused on my body, which kind of ached all over, and my throbbing head.

"Yes."

"What hurts?"

"Everything," I said.

"Let's try to get you up," Gabby said. She reached down and took my arm.

"Wait. Should we move her? What if she broke her neck?" Dad sounded frantic.

"She's fine, Greg. I've seen dozens of kids get thrown from a horse, and she didn't land on her neck. She didn't hit any rocks. She just needs to get her legs back under her. Get her other arm and let's get her up. One, two, three."

I felt myself being pulled from the ground. My dad had a firm hold of me around my waist; otherwise I think I would have sunk down onto the ground again.

My legs felt a little wobbly, but they worked. And it didn't hurt quite as bad as I had thought.

"Walk her around, Greg. Make sure she's okay."

My dad obeyed, but all I could think was that she shouldn't be barking orders at everyone, especially my father. What if I had broken my neck? She would be responsible for me being wheelchair bound for the rest of my life. I had a fleeting thought that it would serve her right, but Dad was pulling at me to walk with him.

\*     \*     \*

"I think you'll be fine, Beka. Do you feel better?" Gabby asked after my dad had checked every joint and made me take a roadside drunk test to prove that I was okay. I was still achy and my head hurt, but I could tell there wasn't any serious damage.

"I guess I'll be fine." I didn't want her getting off the hook too easily. After all, she had chosen the horse.

"Well, let's get these horses back in then. Let me help you back up." Gabby crouched by Thunder's side and laced her fingers into a little step for me.

"I'm not getting back on that thing."

She stood up. "You need to get back on. Just ride him back to the barn."

*Are you crazy? Insane? How could you even suggest that?* I tried to think of something I could say out loud, but I couldn't come up with anything.

"Gabby. Let's just let her walk back on her own. I'll lead her horse." *Thank you, Dad!*

"That's not the point. She needs to get back on so she doesn't develop anxiety about horses," she argued.

"I'm not getting back on," I repeated.

"Beka." She took that parental tone with me, which wouldn't have been a problem if she were actually my parent.

"Look. I got hurt. I'm not riding him."

"But it may make you afraid to ride again. You have to get back on. Give it a try."

"No. Who says I ever want to ride again anyway?"

"Greg?" she pleaded.

"She'll be fine, Gabby. Let's just let it alone." *Strike two!*

She gave us a huffy sigh but went over to help Lucy and Anna mount again. When she got them settled, she came back and took the reins to Dad's horse, after giving him a look that made it clear she wasn't happy with him. Dad came over and took Thunder's bridle.

"You okay, Butterfly?" he asked.

"I think I'll be fine. Thanks."

"No problem," he said. "Let's head on back, pardner." He tipped an imaginary hat at me and then slung his arm around my shoulder. It felt really good.

I popped two Tylenol and showered as soon as I got home. I wanted to get the horse scent off of me. I had messages from Nancy and Lori to return, so I cuddled up on my bed with my phone, and extra pillows to cushion my sore body.

\* \* \*

I decided to call Lori first. I knew Nancy wanted to talk about the retreat, and since I didn't want to, stalling seemed a reasonable tactic.

"So, how'd the trail ride go?" Lori asked.

"Miserable. The horse *she* put me on threw me," I told her.

"I thought you were going to try and be nice to her."

"I tried. I just don't understand why she has to be around at all. It was supposed to be a family ride. She's not family."

Lori was quiet for a few moments. I knew what she was thinking, especially since she had told me several times over the last few weeks to give Gabby a chance, to pray for her, and to trust God for what was going to happen. But I just couldn't stop hating her. I kept imagining her dirty, muddy, twine-tied self smiling and making eyes at my father. It made me seethe inside. She wasn't good enough for my dad, and I didn't want anything to do with her.

"Well," Lori sighed. "You're going to have to make the best of it. It looks like she's going to be around for a while. I know it stinks for you though."

"Some help that is," I pouted.

"Okay, subject swap. Are you going to be gone the entire spring break? I thought maybe we could drive down to the beach or something. I haven't been there yet."

"We?"

"Okay, maybe you could drive and I could sit pitifully in the passenger seat since I don't have my license. You don't have to keep reminding me, ya know."

"I know. I just like teasing. No, we could do that. I leave tomorrow after church and come back Wednesday evening. So I have all day Thursday and Friday until six. We could go on Thursday."

"That would be great. Maybe you should invite Gabby."

"I'm hanging up now . . ."

"Okay, I'll stop. Seriously though, have you even tried to get to know her?"

I took a deep breath, annoyed that she would ask. "Why should I? Dad said they're just friends."

"Well, she's a believer, right?"

"Supposedly."

"Just think about it. Maybe if you got to know her better it wouldn't be so horrible for you when she's around. Besides, it puts you in a bad mood."

"What if I hate her even more?"

"I seriously doubt that would happen. You might even start to like her."

"Okay, keep talking like that and I'll have to find another friend."

"I'm saying it because I am your friend. And besides, with Gretchen on the loose, we may only have each other when we get back to school anyway."

We made plans to meet on Thursday, but the thought of Gretchen returning to school kept spinning webs inside of me. She had been on her very best behavior since her suspension, but she knew I was the one who turned her in for accidentally burning down The Snack Shack. And I knew she wasn't going to let that just slip by. I had the feeling she was purposely trying to torture me by not doing anything, all the while letting me know she was right there, watching, and waiting to pounce.

My real fear was that she had actual ammunition since she had discovered that I stayed at the psychiatric hospital over winter break. Sure, she was popular, and she could sway public opinion about me at school, but now she could make everyone believe that I was certifiably crazy too. And I couldn't get around my shame over it. I really had wanted to kill myself. I thought disappearing would be easier than dealing with all the secrets. Coming clean with my family had helped a lot, starting counseling had helped too, but what was scarier was that life for me was changing again. And once again, I wasn't dealing with it very well.

After my stay at the hospital, I went back to school and had the play going on. It kept me so busy that I barely had time to breathe, much less think. And now there was nothing. It was like a dark vortex returned, taunting me and reminding me that something was still missing. Part of me knew that God was supposed to be filling that hole, but I was so new at the God thing, I didn't always know how to do that. I kind of thought it would be nice to go away for a couple of months and get my footing with God and then return to my life. But instead, it was like trying to climb on a rock that was being battered with wind and waves from every direction. I just couldn't seem to get my footing. And it wasn't just Gabby that bothered me. Or even Gretchen.

It was so much more.

I spotted Nancy as soon as my dad pulled into the church parking lot, and my stomach did a flip. I liked Nancy. She was cheerful and kind, but she was also intimidating. She seemed to have herself so together. And now I would have to spend three nights in a cabin with her. That would probably put an end to the budding friendship.

She was dressed in cargo pants and a tee, and she looked like she could have just finished shooting a commercial for Old Navy. Her smooth blonde hair was pulled back, and her perfect features broke into a wide smile as she trotted up to the car.

"Hey there! Hi, Mr. Madison," she said as Dad and I

climbed out of the car. Dad went around to the back of the car and pulled out my sleeping bag, pillow, and duffel bag.

"Hi. Nancy, right?"

She nodded and shook his hand. "Beka's stuff can go in the blue church van. My dad is one of the drivers, so I made sure that she got assigned to our van." She smiled at me, her eyes telling me that she knew I was nervous. I wasn't sure if it helped. She followed my dad over as he took my bags to the van and threw them on top of the large pile behind the rear seat.

He turned and looked at me. I couldn't read his expression.

"So, Butterfly." He paused for a few minutes and shifted his weight. "Well, I'll see you here on Wednesday night. Have fun."

He gave me a hug but didn't say anything else. It felt awkward because it looked like he wanted to say a lot more.

"Okay, see you Wednesday."

He gave a wave as he went back to the car and left me standing by the blue church van, desperately wishing I could jump back in the car with him and go home.

Then I saw Josh.

And he was headed straight for me.

I straightened up and glanced down to remember what I was wearing, blue capris and a white tee with a scoop neckline. It was simple but flattering. I kicked at the rocks that had broken free from the pavement and tried not to smile too much.

He really was handsome.

He was tall and his dark hair waved slightly as it fell to the right of his forehead. And he had a great tan. I knew my arms were white as snow without even looking at them. The sun did nothing for me except to give me a sunburn or more freckles. Once again I wished I had done something with my plain hair, pulled back in a ponytail again.

"Hey Beka!" he said when he reached me.

"Josh." I nodded and tried to smile a little without looking overeager.

"I'm glad you decided to come. Nancy had said you were on the fence about it."

I took that in and wondered what else Nancy might have told him. Since they were brother and sister I couldn't fault her for talking to him, but it still made me worry.

"Yeah, well, I really didn't enjoy the wilderness thing at Girl Scout camp, so I wasn't sure I wanted to try this." *Why did I have to bring up Girl Scouts?*

"So Paul said he wasn't going to be able to make it."

"My brother the baseball man. He's got practices all week."

We stood there for a minute, the silence growing awkward for me. But Josh didn't seem to mind. He looked me straight in the eye until I had to look down and scuff my foot in the pavement pebbles again.

"So, have you been on these things before?" I asked, glad that my brain had come up with something.

"I usually go every year. Couldn't miss my last year, I figured."

"Oh." I didn't want to ask the question that popped in

my head. I hardly knew Josh at all, but he intrigued me and made my knees go weak. And for some unbelievable reason he had taken an interest in me. He had already asked me to his homeschool formal that was coming up in a month, and he always seemed to single me out in some way. His attention made me feel full inside. But he was finishing up his senior year, which meant, like Paul, college would begin in the fall. Another person I cared about would be leaving. I wouldn't even get a chance to find out if anything could come of it. Whatever *it* was.

But I had to know. If he was leaving, I had to get it in my head that he was only going to be a friend. I shook my head, remembering that I was also going to be going to the junior prom with Mark. Mark. How could I feel things for two guys at once? What was wrong with me?

"So are you going to college in the fall?" I asked.

He broke into a wide grin before he even spoke. "Yep. I got into Seattle Pacific."

My heart dropped to the bottom of my stomach. I forced a smile on my face. "So I guess you're going to Seattle." *Duh. That should put an end to my fanciful thoughts.*

He maintained his grin. "Yeah, I've always wanted to go to Seattle. My family flew out there for a vacation years ago, and I've wanted to go back ever since. It's so beautiful there."

I nodded, unable to form any words. I should have known that I shouldn't get my heart too wound up. I tried to think about Mark, who went to my school, whom I would see practically every day over my senior year. It was much more realistic, and I really liked Mark. But there was just something about Josh. It might be the way he brought God into almost every conversation we had. His relationship with God seemed so natural, and he exuded this confidence and ease with life. Something I knew I didn't have. I shook my head again and pushed the thought away. He would be going to school three thousand miles away. It wasn't even worth thinking about. So why did I still feel sick to my stomach?

"Do you know what you'll study?"

Another grin. *Must be nice to be so sure of things.* "Premed. I want to be a missionary doctor."

"A what?"

"Well, I'm not completely sure yet, but I want to become a doctor so that I can offer to the poor what the rich have at their disposal. I'd love to go on lots of medical mission trips."

I nodded, trying not to look as lost as I felt.

"I'm actually going on one with our church this summer. We're going to Haiti. Dr. Anderson is taking a team down there to run a medical clinic. Did you know people still die of diarrhea down there?"

"No. I guess I didn't know you could die of that." *Okay, now I'm talking about diarrhea with a cute guy. Lovely.*

His eyes were dancing as he continued. "They die because of the dehydration. I'll only be able to help with blood pressures and pulses and things like that, but someday I'll take my own team down there, and to lots of other places too." He paused. "Well, that is, Lord willing."

"That sounds amazing," I said.

"It is. You should come with us. I'm assuming you've never been on a missions trip before, right?"

"No. I mean, I'm just starting to figure out all this God stuff."

"You could at least check it out. We're having an interest meeting in May."

"I'll think about it."

"And we still have a date in May, right?"

I nodded, blushing.

"Good. Well, think about Haiti, really. It'll change your life. I'll catch up with you later."

He waved and walked around to the front of the van. My heart was pounding. He might be going far away, but it wasn't going to be easy to just put him out of my mind.

\*　　　\*　　　\*

Fifteen minutes later I was packed into the rear seat of the van with Nancy on my right, Morgan on my left, and Allison in front of us. I recognized some of the other girls but didn't know them. Morgan had been at a sleepover that Nancy had hosted, so I knew a little bit about her. She had an athletic look; her brown hair was bobbed and she wore jeans with a hooded T-shirt. I also knew she was teased about being boy crazy and that she thought my brother was pretty cute. Apparently she wasn't the only one either.

Allison's wild red hair obscured any view I might have had of the drive, but Nancy and Morgan and Allison kept up a constant chatter on the ninety-minute trip. I didn't really participate except to agree. My head swam with my conversation with Josh for the first half of the trip and then reluctantly turned to what might happen on the retreat.

Fortunately for me, Nancy, Allison, and Morgan's conversation eventually turned to the topic, giving me a heads up about what was coming.

"I think it's just plain cruel that they bring guys on a retreat where we are supposed to focus on purity. Who planned that?" Morgan asked.

"Well, they're coming with us, but they're not going to be with us. I mean, the camp is set up in two sections, with a common area for eating and large group meetings, but mostly we'll be on the girls' side of the camp. At least that's what it sounds like," Nancy explained.

"I thought you'd been on these before," I said.

"I have. We all have been to similar things, but since we have a new youth leader, this one has been planned differently than the ones we've done before. Like usually we just go for Friday and Saturday night and then come back Sunday morning, but this one is three nights, and it's at a different place than we usually go."

It was nice to know I wouldn't be the only one trying to get a feel for things, but I still wasn't convinced I'd survive three nights with everybody.

When we arrived at the camp, the two white vans with the guys turned left down a dirt road while the blue vans continued forward. We were being thrown around in the backseat like popcorn, which even I thought was pretty funny after ten minutes of it. Nancy's dad pulled up alongside a wood cabin that was at the end of a row of identical cabins facing a grassy meadow with other small and large brown buildings dotting the landscape.

When we piled out of the van, Nancy grabbed my arm. "Come on, let's go claim a bed!" she said as she dragged me behind her. Morgan and Allison followed right behind.

I shuddered when I saw where I would be sleeping. The simple cot with the army green blanket on it didn't bother me; it was the fact that the cabin had twelve beds in it, and five girls I had never seen before were already occupying the cots along the far wall. Spending time with girls from my own church was one thing, but now I would have to be around perfect strangers too. I was exhausted just thinking about it. I was going to have to stick close to Nancy and the others. At least with them I wouldn't have to talk very much.

# CHAPTER 4

**Nancy stepped** forward. "C'mon, we can all fit in here." She went up to the first cot and put her sleeping bag on top. "I'll take this one."

I slipped over to the cot next to her, dropping my bags on top. Morgan took the next one, then Allison, and then two girls who must have ridden in the other van claimed the last two. We began unrolling our sleeping bags and stacking our things on the two shelves above each cot. Every five feet along the wall there was a bright green sign that read, "Be aware of the bears! No food in the cabins."

Morgan flopped onto her cot and laced her hands

behind her head. "I just want to announce right now that I snore and there's nothing I can do about it."

"Well, maybe it'll keep the bears away," I said. Morgan laughed.

"I don't care about snoring. I'm just glad there's no school!" Allison said.

"Do you get a break from homeschooling?" I asked Nancy.

"Sort of. I kind of planned to be off this week anyway. It just means I have to work more next week. I think Josh is missing a couple of classes to come though. The community college doesn't have the same break as we do," she said.

"College? I thought Josh was a senior."

"He is technically, but Josh already has his GED. He's taking a lot of his freshman year courses this year, so he can start college as a sophomore."

The screen door slammed and one of our chaperones walked over to the corner. "Okay! Harvest ladies, this way." We all gathered around Dana, who was tiny enough to be engulfed by our small group.

"I think I've met all of you, but I'm Dana. This is my first trip with you guys, so be easy on me, okay?" She handed out a packet of stapled paper to each of us. The top sheet was a map.

"Okay, this is you." She took a red marker and drew a circle around the little drawing of our cabin on each of our papers. "And this," she underlined another little drawing on each of our maps, "is the dining hall. You have to be in the dining hall at 5:00 P.M., but it's only 3:00, so you can do whatever you want for the next two hours.

The yellow sheet in your packet is a list of activities you can choose from. I'm going to be staying in the counselor room in this cabin, so if you need anything, let me know." She took a deep breath and ran her fingers through her short, dark hair. "Any questions? Good. I think I need a nap." Dana disappeared into the bathroom, and I heard a door close.

"That's what I'm going to do," Morgan said.

"What? Sleep? Are you kidding? Let's go find all those guys that supposedly came with us," Allison suggested.

"You guys are hopeless," Nancy said.

We all flipped to our yellow sheets and quietly read them.

"Let's go horseback riding," Nancy said. "They've got a session that starts in twenty minutes. We could make it if we leave now."

"I could do that," Morgan said.

"I should put on some jeans," Allison said.

"That okay with you, Beka?" Nancy asked.

"Oh, I think I'll pass on the horses. Don't worry about me. I'll find something to do," I told her.

"We can't just leave you. Let's find something else." She returned to reading the list.

"No, really. I think I just want to walk around and have some time to myself." When I said it out loud, I actually thought it sounded like the best idea in the whole world. I could only take people for so long before I needed some time away. And judging by the schedule, I wasn't going to get much time alone anyway.

"Are you sure? Because we can."

"Totally sure. Go have fun," I said.

*    *    *

Before they were even finished getting ready, I grabbed my notebook and Bible and headed out the door. I didn't grab the map, but the place didn't seem too complicated. I walked across the field and passed the dining hall where I could smell our dinner being made. I saw other clusters of kids around. On the other side of another field, I could see what I assumed to be the guys' cabins. My thoughts immediately turned to Josh.

And Seattle.

I didn't want to think about him leaving, but it was going to happen whether I thought about it or not. Medical school too. Just like Paul. Why couldn't things just be easy for once? I didn't have any experience with guys, never dated. I didn't know what to do. My head was telling me that I should just let Josh ride off into the sunset, but something about him had me.

I wandered down a small trailhead marked "Beech Bear Trail," and at the end I found a cluster of picnic tables, a fire pit, a set of swings, and a small jungle gym. I walked over to the swings, dropped my notebook onto the ground and set my Bible on it, and sat on a faded blue rubber seat.

I pulled the scrunchie out of my hair and pushed off with my feet, letting the wind blow on my face. Higher and higher I pumped my legs. I felt like I was the only person on earth. I closed my eyes and swung, letting the rhythm of the swing settle my heart. Letting the cool

April air clear my head. It was times like this I couldn't formulate words to pray. But I knew I wasn't alone. I smiled as I imagined God giving me a push on the swing. A push. Maybe that's what I needed. A push in one direction or the other. A deliberate move toward something. I felt like I was just watching life happen around me.

I scuffed my sneakers in the dirt to slow the swing down. The peace I had felt in the air now thudded into reality. But I didn't feel like leaving either. I so wanted God to talk to me. I wanted to be sure of something, anything. I rested my face on the chain and swung gently in a small circle. It seemed to be the perfect place to just wait.

\*     \*     \*

The sky had turned into a deep blue with just a hint of red above the trees in front of me. I hadn't worn my watch, but I knew I hadn't been gone very long. I still had time to rest. I leaned back in the seat and let my hair drag on the ground. I had to do something about my hair. But if I cut it now it would look like I was copying Lucy. Maybe I could . . .

"I didn't expect to find you here."

I knew that voice. I took a deep breath and pulled myself upright. Sure enough, Josh was walking right toward me.

"I didn't expect to be found." I didn't know whether to stay in the swing or stand up.

He walked around behind me and pulled back gently on the chains and then let them go. "I loved the swings when I was little." I felt his hands on my back as he pushed me higher and higher. I barely breathed.

"Me too. Paul and I used to swing as high as we could then jump off to see who could jump the farthest. He always won."

"Figures. How far apart are you two?"

"Almost eighteen months. We did everything together." Even Josh's strong hands and his presence couldn't push away the sadness that swept in. Paul would be leaving, and nothing would ever be the same.

Josh stopped pushing and came around and leaned on the metal support next to my swing. I walked my feet in the dirt to stop the swing and stood up. He was taller than I was, but I didn't have to look up quite as much.

"You look sad," he said. He wrinkled his dark eyebrows slightly.

"Am I that transparent?" I walked over to one of the picnic tables and sat down. He followed and sat down across from me. I forced myself to take a deep breath. I still couldn't believe it was him that showed up. Out of all the people at the camp, out of everybody who could have wandered back here, Josh was with me.

And I couldn't help but wonder if this was the push I was looking for.

"You just seemed sad all of a sudden, that's all." He rested his elbows on the table and leaned forward.

"Oh. Well." It wasn't really any of his business, and I wasn't in the habit of sharing my thoughts. But something about the place we were in, the quietness. It didn't seem weird at all.

"Paul's going to be leaving. It just stinks. I mean, I

want him to go. But I don't want him to go," I said.

"I know what you mean. I'm really excited about Seattle but . . ." He took a deep breath and blew it out slowly. "But it's gonna be hard to leave." He lowered his eyes and then lifted them to meet mine.

I took a deep breath too. That image of Josh disappearing into the sunset came back to me. There just didn't seem to be anything to say.

"Enough of this. We better walk back for dinner. We'll have more time to talk." He smiled and stood up. I stood up and walked next to him, but halfway down the trail I stopped.

"I left my stuff. My Bible and notebook are by the swings." I turned to head back, and he took my arm. His hand sent flutters through every nerve in my skin and straight into my heart.

"I'll get them. Wait right here."

He took off at a jog back the way we had just come. All he did was touch my arm and my heart was beating a mile a minute. I took some deep breaths to try and get ahold of myself. What was wrong with me?

By the time he trotted back I was composed, but the thought of him kissing me flitted through my mind. *Where did that come from?* And here I was at a purity retreat. Morgan was right. It was just plain cruel to have the guys here at all.

\*     \*     \*

We didn't talk on the way back, but it was nice just knowing he was next to me. We walked into the dining hall together, and when I spotted Nancy, Morgan, and Allison, I could tell they noticed.

"It looks like people are sitting with their cabins," Josh said as he looked around. Was he disappointed?

"Yeah, I see Nancy and the others." I didn't move.

"See you later?" he asked. Most people said see you later as a good-bye, but he was asking.

I smiled. "Sure. Later."

He smiled back and then turned toward the left side of the room. I left for my table, my heart still fluttering ever so slightly, but I wasn't worried about them hearing my heart. It was my hot cheeks I was worried about. And I couldn't just blush sweetly, I had to get red and blotchy. And the closer I got to the table the blotchier I felt.

So how was your horseback ride?" I asked when I sat down next to Nancy.

"Apparently not as interesting as your afternoon." Allison lowered her chin and raised her eyebrows at me.

Nancy didn't say anything.

"We just ran into each other at the playground and walked back here. No big deal."

An announcer in the front of the room asked for everybody's attention as he blessed the food. After the prayer, I slid a glance at Nancy, who focused on passing food around the table.

"So did you have fun?" I tried again.

"Yeah, it was nice. I've only ever done pony rides at

the fair, so it was pretty cool," she answered.

I lowered my voice and leaned over. "Are you mad?"

"Why, is there something to be mad about?"

"I don't know. You just seem upset."

She finished getting her salad and then passed the bowl. She stared at her plate for a minute before she looked up.

"I guess I just don't want him to get hurt," she said.

"Hurt? Who me? We barely know each other."

"He's leaving, Beka."

"I know."

"Well."

"Well, what do you want me to do?" My voice went up, and Allison and Morgan looked over. We waited a moment until Morgan and Allison returned to their conversation.

"Look, Nancy, there's nothing going on. We were just talking. I promise."

"I know." She smiled sadly. "But you're going to that dance too. It just worries me."

"Why?" I pressed.

"Because Josh never goes to those things. And this year he's going. With you."

"Maybe it's just because it's his last year, you know."

She raised her eyebrows. "Sure."

I didn't know what else to say, but I didn't want things to get weird with Nancy over it. And I wasn't about to give up Josh either. I spent the rest of the meal feeling awkward and guilty, desperately wishing I could just go home.

\*　　　\*　　　\*

Once the main session was over with, we were given until ten to be back at our bunks for a small group time.

"What should we go do?" Morgan asked as we walked out of the meeting hall.

"I heard they have a game room. Let's go hang out there," Allison said.

Everybody agreed, but I wondered where Josh was. I knew I shouldn't spend the whole time wondering where he might be, but I couldn't help myself. Nancy checked her map and led us toward the game room.

It was a bright green and blue room that was about half the size of the large dining hall. The corner closest to us had a cluster of couches, as well as tables and chairs set up. Three large bookshelves were filled with games and puzzles. At the other end of the room there were several pool tables, foosball tables, and what looked like an air hockey machine. Even though there were a bunch of other kids there already, it took only one quick scan of the room to see that Josh wasn't there.

I felt like a deflated balloon. Which was ridiculous, especially since there was nothing going on. Right?

We went over to the bookshelves and found a game to play, but before we had the game unpacked, Josh walked in. He looked around and then caught my eye. He smiled and walked over to our table.

"Hey Sis," he said as he grabbed Nancy's shoulders.

"Hey," she said, tilting her head back to look up at him. "You want to play?"

My heart raced.

"Nah. Why don't you all come play pool?"

"Okay. That okay?" Nancy looked around the table.

Morgan shrugged. "Fine by me."

"I don't know how to play," Allison said.

"You'll figure it out," Nancy said.

We put the game away then followed Josh to the back of the room to claim a table. A big, round guy with a dirty T-shirt came up to Josh just as we were about to start. He had sweat dripping from his forehead, and his thin hair was wet on top.

"Hey Josh! Mind if I play?" The guy looked around at all of us but gave an extra big smile to Nancy. It was so obvious I almost laughed. Nancy smiled back but quickly said, "Well, if we can round up one more guy, then we'll play guys against girls. Allison can just be extra for us."

"I don't care if I just watch. I think I might hurt somebody with that big stick. I tend to talk with my hands, ya know," Allison said. She climbed onto a stool near the wall.

"Hey Scott! Do you wanna play?" Josh called out to a group of guys over by the couches playing some video games.

A tall blond guy with a fabulous tan stood up and walked over to us. He smiled at Nancy too. We played for almost an hour, but Josh seemed to treat everybody nicely, and didn't single me out once. By the end I was getting irritated. With myself, with him. Maybe I really was reading too much into the whole thing. Even when we all had to go back to our bunks, he waved at everybody with a general good-bye. I don't know what I expected exactly, but I was disappointed.

\*     \*     \*

By lunchtime the next day, I was sick of hearing about purity and sex. I had no plans to have sex, so I just felt like it was a waste of time. Mostly anyway; after all, there was still a chance to see Josh now and then. But when the afternoon speaker started, I was too scared not to listen. It was like he was reading my thoughts.

"Some of you may think you don't need to be here. You're not dating, you're not interested in starting a sex life, you may even have already made a commitment to stay pure for your future mate. But I want to ask you this. Of the twenty-four hours you have in a day, how much of the time do you spend thinking about some guy or some girl?" He waited for a minute and then added, "Now. How much time do you spend thinking about God?"

I didn't even want to do the calculation.

He went on for forty-five minutes, and by the end I knew I had some serious thinking to do. God came into my life around the same time Mark did. And then I met Josh, and between Josh and Mark I spent a lot of time thinking about them both. Going back and forth, asking lots of questions that I didn't have answers for. Was Josh or Mark an idol though? Just because I thought about them? Or because I was so preoccupied with seeing them or being near them that my thoughts about God even centered on them. Ughhhh. Didn't God understand, though? He knows I'm a teenage girl. And I was doing a lot less than most teenage girls. My thoughts went to Gretchen and her well-known reputation. In comparison, I thought I was doing pretty well.

It was just too much to take in. I didn't even want to think about it.

And all my thoughts flew out of my head when Josh walked toward me after the 1:00 session ended.

He barely paused, but he whispered, "Will you meet me by the swings during the break?"

"Sure." I tried to sound casual, glad that he couldn't hear my heart fluttering. He kept walking, and I could barely wait to get there.

*       *       *

When I stepped into the clearing, he was already there, sitting at one of the picnic tables just as we had the day before. I walked over to the table and sat down across from him.

"What do you think of the retreat so far?" he asked.

The only word that popped in my head was "idolatry." Not what I wanted to think about.

I shrugged. "It's okay, I guess."

He smiled and when he did I noticed that he had a really small dimple on his right cheek. Why hadn't I seen that before?

"The speakers have been great. I guess I was kind of worried about you—being new at this and all. It's a lot to take in."

"Too much," I said, blowing out the breath I had been holding.

He looked around. "Now that I think about it, we probably should have met in the common area or something. Do you want to walk back?"

*Why? We just got here!* I thought. But I couldn't make the question come out of my mouth. Maybe I didn't really want to know why. Maybe he was just trying to be polite. I remembered how Mark had confessed how he felt about me when we were alone at a picnic table. It just seemed like another great moment in the works, but now Josh wanted to leave.

I didn't answer but I stood up.

He stood and said, "I want to keep talking, but maybe we should just go somewhere more public."

We started walking and I finally blurted out, "Why? We're not doing anything but talking."

He stopped and turned to me and put his hand on my elbow. No chills this time. He looked too serious. "Oh, I know. But it wouldn't look right. And people could assume we were doing something wrong. And here of all places. It just wouldn't look right."

I turned and started walking on the trail again.

"You're the one that told me to meet you here." *I don't understand!*

He caught up with me and put his hand on my shoulder to stop me. "I'm sorry, Beka. Really. I should have thought it through better. I just saw you after that session and this was the first place that came to mind. I'm sorry."

I nodded, and we walked the rest of the way in silence. I was hurt. I couldn't help it. I felt like something was wrong with me. Girls met guys, started dating, and had boyfriends all the time. What was wrong with me? Why was I interested in these guys who were more confused than I was?

\*      \*      \*

There was a common area right outside the meeting hall that had a small garden in the center with faded wood benches. He led us over to one and sat down. I flopped onto the bench, unable to hide my emotions. Paul used to say that he never wondered what I was feeling—it was why that he never understood. Josh seemed to know too.

"I really am sorry."

"I know." I didn't look up. But then I thought that since he was leaving, what did I have to lose by being honest?

"I feel like you don't trust me."

"You? No, I don't always trust myself. And I know how people talk. If we keep things out in the open, then there won't be any questions."

"Keep what out in the open?"

He paused for a minute, long enough for me to feel uncomfortable waiting for an answer.

"Getting to know each other. Becoming friends."

So that's all it was. Not bad. But it wasn't much. I didn't know how to respond.

"I know I'm leaving in August, but there's still some time."

"Three thousand miles, Josh. I'm not sure I see the point. You're great and all but . . ." *But maybe I need to let it go.* It felt dangerous. Like I was bound to get my heart broken in all of this somewhere.

"We can still keep in touch," he offered.

Did I want to? Did I want to develop a friendship with someone who was going to leave? Especially when I knew my emotions were already too involved? Was it worth the risk? I felt like I was back on Thunder, wanting to stop and get off, but finding myself along for the ride. I just hoped I wouldn't find myself thudding to the ground this time.

As soon as I got home Wednesday evening, I went straight to the shower. I felt grimy after three mornings of showering in water so cold I could barely stand to get under it. And my hair hadn't been washed well in days. Since no one was fighting to get in the bathroom, I stayed in there for as long as I could, letting the warm water spray my face.

I thought about how Dad had asked me about the retreat the minute I climbed into the car.

"It was fine," I answered.

"Fine? Do you want to be more specific?"

I shrugged. "Sometimes it was fun. Sometimes it was confusing. Mostly it was overwhelming. That enough of an answer?" I leaned back on the seat and closed my eyes. I wasn't trying to be mean, but I didn't want to talk about it.

"Why was it overwhelming?" he asked, not getting the hint.

"Daa-ad. It just was."

"Well, when you feel like talking about it, I'd like to hear about it." He cleared his throat, and I could hear the leather of his seat squeak as he shifted his weight. I opened my eyes a crack and looked over at him.

"I know your mom talked to you, well . . . discussed . . . she went over, I think . . . that stuff."

"Not you too! Dad, they've been talking about sex all weekend. Can we give it a break?"

"Sure, it's just . . ." He shifted again. "I don't know how far she got."

"All the way, Dad. I even know that you two did it."

His eyes got round.

"Dad, relax. It's no big deal. You don't have to worry about me. You should worry about Anna. She's the one you're going to have to talk to."

He groaned. "I know." He turned and looked at me. "You think Lucy . . . umm."

"Yes, Lucy knows."

Dad shook his head. "I miss your mom anyway, but I really miss her when it comes to this stuff."

The obvious question popped into my head. Would he think about getting married again? I was too afraid to ask.

*     *     *

As I combed out my hair after my thirty-minute shower, I was still thinking about it. I don't think I was so against my dad ever getting married again. It was more that I didn't want him to marry Gabby—ever. My counselor Julie wouldn't be a bad idea. She wasn't married, and she was smart and stylish and really nice. I had only been seeing her for a few months, but I trusted her. The more I thought about it, the better it sounded. Julie would be perfect for Dad. Now if only Dad would be willing to give someone else a try. There had to be a way to get them together long enough for him to learn more about her. I wasn't sure if she was seeing anyone. But I had never seen pictures of any guys, so that was a good sign. I was going to have to think about that. I tossed the hairbrush in the sink and ran back to my room. I had to call Lori.

"So what do you think?" I asked when I had finished. She had barely said hello when I launched into my idea.

"You want to set your dad up with your counselor? Are you serious?"

"Why not? I think it'd be a great match."

"It's not that. It's just, well, he might not like it very much if . . ."

"If he marries someone, then she'll be my step-mother. That affects my life. I should have some kind of say in it, shouldn't I?"

"Don't get mad. I'm just saying that he might not appreciate you meddling with his love life."

"Whatever." My good mood was now gone.

"Hey, are we still going to the beach tomorrow?" Lori asked.

"I don't know."

"I'm sorry, Beka. I shouldn't have said anything. I guess it couldn't hurt to see what happens between them."

"That's all I'm saying. What could it hurt?" I still wasn't happy, but I agreed to pick her up to go to the beach.

*　　*　　*

When I knocked on Lori's door the next morning, Megan answered with a bright smile.

"Beka! Good to see you. Come on in, Lori's still upstairs." Megan led me into their family room. I sat down but didn't know what to say. I kind of just sat there smiling stupidly. Megan sat down across from me on the couch. The same spot she had been when she had told Lori and me about Jesus. I thought back to that afternoon, remembering how real God had felt. And realizing how, even at the retreat, I felt like I was struggling to get that feeling back again.

"So where are you two going?" she asked. Megan was now officially Lori's mom, since the adoption was finalized.

"Just down to Little River Inlet," I told her.

"Oh, that'll be nice. I was wondering if you had thought any more about working in my studio this summer. I could use some help."

"Really?" I asked.

She nodded. She had asked me already, but I hadn't pursued it because I thought she was just being nice.

"What would I do?"

"Well, I need help answering the phone and scheduling appointments, but if you're interested in learning more about photography, you could help me with some of the family sessions too."

Dad had never brought up working last summer since Mom had just died, but I knew he'd like the idea. I wondered if Lori would mind me working for her new mom.

"Sorry!" Lori said as she came around the corner. "I got in the shower late." The smile Lori and Megan exchanged made my heart ache. "Are you okay, Beka?"

"Me? Oh, I'm fine. I was just thinking. Megan said she needed help at her studio."

"Are you going to do it? It would be so cool. I'd work there too except I'm going to take some college classes this summer," Lori said.

"College classes? Why?" It was the first I had heard of it.

She perched on the edge of one of the chairs. "We just figured it all out this week. I want to take some more languages, and they offer Russian and Chinese over at the community college."

"Wow." It was all I could come up with.

"Well, let's go. I'm dying to see the beach," Lori said.

"Don't be too disappointed. We're only going to be on the bay."

"Oh, I know, but there will still be water and sand. That's all I need." Lori got up and Megan and I followed her to the door.

"Oh, before you go, Lori tells me that you both got

invited to a formal next month. I thought we could all go shopping together to get your dresses if you'd like."

"Really?" A lump instantly formed in my throat and my eyes stung as tears bubbled up. I swallowed hard and tried to steady my voice. "Well, I still need to ask my dad if I can go. But I'd like that."

"And we can get ready over here too," Lori said. "Mom can help us with our hair and take pictures and all of that stuff. What do ya think?"

"That sounds great." I bit the back of my lip to keep the tears from spilling over.

As we climbed into the car, I couldn't decide if I wanted to cry or laugh. I had spent some time praying just that morning. Actually, it wasn't so much praying as it was complaining. I had been telling God that I felt weird about looking for a dress and getting ready for a dance without my mom to help me. And even though we had been having trouble when she died, I knew she would have been thrilled to do that mother-daughter stuff with me. And then this. Out of nowhere help comes. God had just answered my prayers. He really was listening.

\*     \*     \*

"I just don't know what to make of it," I told Lori as we sat on a big piece of driftwood at the base of the dune.

"Seattle's a long way away," she said.

"Doesn't it make it pointless?"

"Kind of." She took a deep breath. "I wish I knew

what to tell you. Have you prayed about it?"

"Yeah. Sort of. I don't know. I don't even know what I want anymore. I like Josh. But Mark's right here." I pushed my bare feet into the sand and then pulled my toes up until I could just see the bright pink polish on my toes.

"Well, I don't think you have to figure out what you want and then ask God. Maybe you should ask God what He wants for you."

"What if He doesn't want what I want?" I asked.

Lori turned and looked at me. She smiled sadly.

I stood up with a sigh and walked down to the water. Tiny waves lapped at my feet. The water was ice cold. A few minutes later Lori appeared next to me.

"I don't know what to tell you. Maybe you just need to stop worrying about it? Go to the dance with Josh and the prom with Mark. Have fun. See what happens."

"Sounds easy, doesn't it? I hate this sometimes. Not knowing what's coming. But with Josh going to Seattle, that kind of answers the question, right? Mark makes sense for right now. It's not like I'm getting married anyway, right?"

"I still think you need to let go. Mark worries me, Bek. You can do whatever you want, but I don't trust him."

"You don't know him," I argued.

"I know enough. Just be careful with him," she said.

I didn't feel like arguing with her. The day was not turning out like I wanted. I thought having God in my life would make things less confusing instead of more confusing.

"I love this place." She took a deep breath. "You can

smell the ocean. The wind, the sand. It's wonderful."

"A lot of the kids hang out here." I pointed to my right. "That bonfire pit is the site of many Bragg County parties. I've only been to one of them. I know Gretchen comes here a lot during the summer with her friends."

"Gretchen. Now there's something to worry about," Lori said.

I groaned. "I can't think about it. It makes me sick. I told you she knows about the hospital." I threw up my hands. "You're right. I probably won't need to worry about Mark. Because he's going to find out I'm a mental patient, and he won't want anything to do with me."

"What do you think will happen? I mean, really?" Lori folded her arms and started chewing on her thumbnail.

"With Gretchen? Who knows? But she's not going to just let it slip by, I can tell you that."

"Looks like a storm. Should we go?" Lori pointed out to our left where the sky was growing dark.

"Yeah, we might as well," I said. We walked up to the bonfire pit to get our shoes and then walked back up to the parking lot. I wished spring break could last forever.

The house was unusually quiet when I got home. It was warm and dark, and I could hear the rain pounding on the roof. I walked back to the family room where my dad was sitting in his recliner, the floor lamp next to him casting an easy glow in the room.

"You're soaked," he said, taking off his glasses and putting his book aside.

"Yeah, it's pouring. Where is everybody?"

"Let's see. Paul is at baseball practice, Anna's with Gabby, and Lucy's at the gym. Do you want some hot chocolate? I'll make some."

"Sure. I'll go get changed." I gave him a hug when he stood up. "Thanks."

*     *     *

I ran up to my room and changed into a pair of pajama pants and a T-shirt. I combed out my hair in the bathroom for a few minutes. It was the perfect time to talk to him about the dances if I could just work up the courage.

When I went back down, the kitchen was bright and my dad was getting the mugs ready. It looked like night-time outside even though it was only three in the afternoon.

"Whipped cream?" he asked, holding up the can.

"Definitely." I climbed onto one of the stools across from the stove top and put my chin in my hands.

"So. How're things going?" he asked.

"Well. There's actually something I wanted to talk to you about."

"Shoot." He set the mugs aside while the water heated up.

"Okay. Well, I got invited to go to a dance. With a guy." I watched my dad's face. His shoulders squared a bit, and I could see him taking in a long deep breath.

"I need more information," he said.

I explained who Josh was and about the dance. "Paul knows Josh if you want to ask him. I really want to go," I finished.

The tea kettle started whistling, and Dad took a few minutes pouring the hot chocolate, stirring it, and adding the whipped cream. He slid the penguin mug over to me and then sat down on one of the stools across from me.

"How well do you know this young man?" he asked. He was using his "dad" voice.

"Not real well. But he's Nancy's older brother—you like her. And Paul knows Josh. You've probably even met him before. And how can I get to know somebody if I don't go out anywhere?"

"Now hold on. I haven't said no. I'm just trying to find out everything I can."

I took a sip from my drink and tried to relax. I put the mug down. "If it would make you feel better, we can probably double with Lori and Brian."

"I would be happier if you were in a group, yes."

"So I can go?"

"I'd like to talk to Paul first and see what he thinks of Josh."

"That's fine. Paul likes him." I took a few more sips of my hot chocolate. I wasn't sure whether to bring up the junior prom yet or not. It could backfire to ask, especially when there were two different guys involved. I decided to tackle one at a time. After all, the junior prom wasn't until the beginning of June.

The back door swung open, and the sound of the rain flooded the kitchen until the door shut. We could hear someone taking off their jacket and shoes, and a moment later Paul appeared around the corner.

"Hey! What are you guys doing?" Paul asked.

I held up my mug. "You want some hot chocolate?" I asked.

"Yeah, that sounds great." He went over and got another mug down while Dad got the chocolate ready.

"Practice was cut short?" Dad asked.

"Coach let us go after he realized it wasn't going to stop. Some of the guys went to the cages, but I'm whipped."

"Your timing is good. Beka and I were just talking about a dance that's coming up. What's your opinion of . . . Josh, is it?"

I held my breath. I wish he had brought it up when I wasn't sitting in the room. It was embarrassing. Paul stirred his drink slowly.

"Josh is a good guy," he finally said.

"You wouldn't be worried about him taking Beka out?" Dad asked.

"Not about Josh. But I can't say I'm not worried. She's my sister. I think you should keep her locked up until she's at least twenty-one."

Dad laughed and then Paul joined in.

"Look, you two. Can you just tell me if I can go, Dad?"

"If Paul thinks this guy is okay, then I'll say yes, but I want you to go with other people, not by yourself. And I still want to meet him."

"Simple. He goes to our church. You can meet him anytime."

Dad nodded slowly. "That's fine." He took a really deep breath. "I knew this would come someday but . . . you guys are just growing up too fast."

Dad and Paul started talking about baseball again, so I slipped up to my room. I was glad about Josh, but I knew the conversation about Mark wasn't going to be as easy. I thought maybe I should try to talk to Paul before I talked to Dad, to get a feel for what he'd tell Dad, even though I already knew what he would probably say. Maybe I could convince him to trust me despite what he'd heard.

*　　*　　*

Lori was busy the rest of spring break, so I spent the last couple of days dwelling on the thought of facing Gretchen. At church they had brought up the idea of praying for our enemies. Lori had talked about it back when Gretchen was slandering her, and I knew the verse anyway, but praying for Gretchen wasn't something I was much interested in doing. And I was seriously considering how I could avoid her altogether. The thought of people, especially Mark, finding out about my hospitalization made me feel sick inside. And I knew it was going to happen. It was a question of when, and how.

*　　*　　*

Lori was waiting at my locker Monday morning. Instead of her usual big grin, she looked serious and smiled half-heartedly when she saw me.

"You okay?" I asked.

She shrugged. "Yeah." She shifted her backpack on her shoulder. "You know, it's been almost a month since the play and Gretchen hasn't done a thing. Maybe there's nothing to worry about," she said as I unpacked my bag.

Something *was* wrong. I could tell. But honestly I was more worried about my own problems at the moment. "But that's why I'm getting worried. She hasn't done anything and she's not going to ignore the fact that I turned her in to the police. No, she's plotting, trust me. And the waiting is almost worse. My mind's going nuts—what is she going to do? What's going to happen? Honestly, I wish there was a way I could just disappear." I closed my locker and knocked my forehead against it. I heard Lori sigh and fall against the locker next to me.

"What am I gonna do?" I asked.

"I don't know," she said. "Just try not to think about it. It's not going to do any good to freak out about it, 'cause you don't know if anything's going to happen."

"But I do know."

"Gretchen's on probation. She's a smart girl. Why would she risk it?"

"Because she can destroy my life without getting in trouble herself. All she has to do is spread the rumor about me and that'll be it. I can't talk about it anymore." I pushed away from my locker.

"See you in second," Lori called down the hallway. I lifted my hand to acknowledge her but kept walking. She had only had a taste of Gretchen's wrath. She had no idea what I could be in for.

\*　　\*　　\*

Gretchen was already in second period when I got there. She was twisting one of her short blonde curls as she smiled and talked to a couple of other girls nearby. I took a deep breath and walked in. She straightened when she saw me and sat back in her chair.

"Hey Beka," she said. She didn't exactly smile, but she wasn't scowling either.

"Hey," I said. I slipped into my seat, and she turned back to talk to her friends.

*What was that?* I turned to catch Lori's eye and she smiled and shrugged. I didn't even hear the rest of the class. I was too busy trying to figure out what Gretchen was up to.

At lunch, Lori suggested that maybe Gretchen had given up and realized that I had no choice but to turn her in.

"Sure. No, something's up. Why would she be nice to me?"

"Beka, you're overanalyzing it. You've got to stop worrying about it. There's probably nothing to worry about anyway," she said.

If only it were that easy.

\*     \*     \*

Ms. Adams sat us down for a meeting in journalism to hand out new assignments. Gretchen had waved once and smiled twice. I was beyond confused.

"Okay, the Young Believers Club is doing a program on abstinence during the Family Life portion of Health sometime next week. Any volunteers?" Ms. Adams asked. Everyone was quiet.

"Beka would be perfect for that assignment. You're into that kind of stuff, aren't you, Beka?" Gretchen turned and smiled again. The whole class was staring at me, and I could feel my cheeks burning.

"You up for it, Beka?" Ms. Adams was all business today and didn't seem to notice that the whole thing was totally bizarre.

"Sure," I managed to squeak out. Ms. Adams immediately turned to the next assignment, taking everyone's attention with her. I let out the breath I had been holding. Gretchen didn't turn around again during the meeting, but when it was over she walked up to me before I had even stood up.

"Hope you don't mind me volunteering you for that assignment." She cocked her head at me. I couldn't tell if she was being serious or sarcastic.

"No. That's fine." It was almost like the last six weeks hadn't even happened.

"Good. I just thought you'd be the best one to talk about the 'no sex' thing." She walked off toward the computers where Mai was waiting for her. Gretchen leaned over and said something to Mai, and Mai flicked her eyes over to where I was unfortunately still staring at them. I looked down and stuffed my notes into a folder and then shoved my stuff into my bag. I had to get out of there. I had to get somewhere where I could clear my head and think. I asked Ms. Adams if I could go to the bathroom and hurried out.

I knew Mark was in music theory during seventh, so I walked down to the band wing, not even sure what I wanted to ask him. I could hear lots of different music coming from different parts of the hallway. I walked by three different rehearsal rooms and then in the fourth one, there he was, sitting with his guitar and singing. The song was gentle and sweet, and I couldn't move as I watched him.

Suddenly he stopped and looked up. He didn't seem surprised to see me.

"Hey Beautiful." He smiled and snapped his head back. "Come on in."

I walked into the small room and
sat down in one of the other folding chairs, dropping my
bag by my feet.

Mark smiled and then looked down at the guitar and
began to play again.

He sang, "Does it seem, too much to ask, to have you
stay, by my side, by my heart?" He stopped and looked
up at me again. "Cutting?"

"Sort of. I'm supposed to be in the bathroom, I guess."

"What's up?"

"I don't know."

He strummed the guitar slowly, just looking at me.
He stopped and held it out. "Wanna try it?"

"Sure." I took the guitar and held it in my lap. Mark stood up and walked behind me, laying his arms and hands across mine. I'm sure he could hear my heart thumping. He slid the pick into my right hand and curled the fingers of my left hand around the arm of the guitar. He positioned my fingers on the strings and pressed them in, then took my right hand and strummed the strings. It sounded good.

"You'll have to cut those nails if you want to learn to play," he said.

I looked at my nails. "All of them?"

"Just your left hand, so you can press the strings."

"That'll look lovely. I'd just have to cut them all."

"Now you try," he said.

I put my fingers back where they had been and strummed the strings. It sounded bad. He leaned over to look at my fingers and repositioned them. I could smell his hair and hear his breath. He was close enough to kiss. Mark turned, his lips inches from mine. "Try again," he said.

I strummed. It sounded better. Mark walked back to the other chair and slid into it.

"I could teach you, you know. If you're interested."

I looked at the guitar and then back up at him.

"I'm interested. But I don't have a guitar."

"There are rehearsal ones here you can use. We can practice after school. Besides, it would give us more time together." He grinned and moved his foot next to mine. The room felt warm all of a sudden. I curled my fingers back in the position he showed me and tried again.

"What were you singing before?" I asked.

"Just a song I'm writing," he said.

I strummed the strings, and he leaned forward to fix my fingers again.

"It's beautiful. I didn't know you could write songs."

"You could too. It's not hard once you learn the basics. But you'd have to get your own guitar to practice."

"I could ask for one for my birthday." I laid the guitar flat in my lap to get a good look at it. It felt different to have it in my arms.

"Hmmm. A birthday, huh? Seventeen? When?"

"May 23rd."

The bell rang and the hallway outside the rehearsal room door flooded with kids. I picked up the guitar and held it out to him. "Thanks. I better go find my brother."

"Can I take you home?"

I thought quickly. Could I pull it off? "Maybe. I have to let my brother know I'm not going with him."

"I'll wait for you then. My car's parked along the back row to the left."

I grinned. "Okay. See ya." I grabbed my bag and left, my mind spinning. What could I tell Paul without actually lying? I stopped by my locker, but even after getting my stuff and walking all the way down to where Paul's locker was, I still didn't have any ideas.

"Hey Bek!" I turned to see Paul jogging toward me. "I've got practice today. You can take the car home." He tossed the keys through the air.

I caught them and tossed them back as he passed me. Paul turned and jogged backwards, lifting his hands to ask why.

"I've got a ride. You can keep the car here."

"You sure?" he asked.

"Yeah. I'm fine."

"Okay. Later." He turned and kept jogging down the hallway.

Perfect.

*　　*　　*

I could see Mark smiling through the windshield as I walked around to the passenger side and got into his little black Celica.

"Where to?" he asked.

I shrugged. "Just take me away."

"No problem." Mark pulled out of the parking lot and got onto the highway. He didn't say much else and I was glad. I didn't feel like talking and I didn't feel like thinking. Before long I could tell we were headed to Little River Inlet. He pulled into Dune Lot #6, the very end of the road, just where Lori and I had been last week.

"Bonfire Beach. I thought you were a mountain guy," I said.

"Sometimes. But today is beautiful, you're beautiful, and the beach seemed perfect."

That was the second time he had called me beautiful, and for the second time I let the comment pass. No one but my dad had ever said that to me.

We climbed out of the car and walked down to where the beach started. He climbed over some large pieces of driftwood used to keep the sand out of the parking lot, and then he turned and offered me his hand.

I took it to climb over, but when I landed on the other side he didn't let go, he just led me down to the bonfire pit. He sat down and pulled me next to him and then laced his fingers through mine.

"I'm glad you could come," he said.

"I can't stay long, really."

"So what's going on today? You've been kind of quiet."

"Gretchen."

"Ahhh. What is it now?"

"She's being nice," I said.

"And?" Mark turned toward me a little more.

"And? That's it. She's being nice. I turn her in to the police, she glares at me for weeks, and then all of a sudden she's being nice. I don't get it."

"You're asking the wrong person about that. I don't even pretend to understand you females."

I grinned. "What? Too much for you?"

"Sometimes." He reached over and picked up some of my hair and then let it fall through his fingers. I thought we were joking, but he seemed too serious all of a sudden.

He took my hand again and rubbed his thumb on mine, staring at me. He slowly began to lean toward me, and with his other hand he reached for my waist.

"Whoa, there," I said. I blocked his hand and let go of the other one.

"What?"

"What? What are you doing?"

"I thought we could, you know, get to know each other a little better."

75

"Mark, we talked about this. You're the one who wanted to be friends."

"But we're going to the prom; I'm sure my parents are backing off. It's just a matter of time."

"Before what? We can get to know each other, Mark. I'd love to know what goes on in your head and listen to you sing and lots of things, but let's cool the contact. It makes me feel like that's all you want."

"It's not all I want." He seemed offended.

"Well, why are you always trying then?"

"Why are you always pushing me away?"

"This is crazy, Mark. What are we doing?"

"You found me, remember?"

"I know. But I needed a friend. I don't need to make out." I stood up and walked toward the water. I could hear him following me.

"Look, Beka, I'm sorry, alright." He turned me toward him and brushed the hair off my face. "I just want to be near you. I'll wait till you're ready. I promise."

*Ready for what?* I wondered. We walked back to the car and climbed in. I wanted to ask him a million more questions, but they were all stuck in my throat. I wished I had listened a little better on that retreat. It seemed like he could be talking about something more than what I would ever be ready for. He had told me about a relationship he had the previous summer with a girl, and how they had slept together and she had gotten pregnant. She ended up miscarrying and his parents had forbidden him to date. I knew in my heart they wouldn't approve of us hanging out alone together, and there was no question about what my dad would think. I looked over at him as he drove, his thick wavy hair, bright blue eyes. What was wrong with me? Here was this cute guy interested in me and I kept pushing him away.

I knew I wasn't comfortable with the physical stuff simply because I had never had a boyfriend to get physical with. I didn't know how I really felt about it morally. The subject hadn't come up. Was it wrong to kiss a guy? Should I not have let him hold my hand? It was so much more complicated than "don't have sex." I seriously hadn't thought it was an issue I had to worry about. And now it clouded every thought.

Mark pulled onto my street, and when he got close to my house, I saw my dad's SUV in the driveway. I glanced down at my watch. He was early.

"Pull over here," I said. "You can't pull in the driveway."

Mark pulled over and I grabbed my bag.

"Thanks for the ride." I turned to get out, but he grabbed my hand and pulled me back to look at him.

"Are we okay?" he asked.

"Sure. Why?"

"You've been quiet. I'm sorry. I won't push, okay. I just want to be with you."

"I've got to go." I glanced at the house, wondering if my dad could see me.

"Can I see you this weekend?" he asked.

"I don't know how."

"If I can figure it out?"

"I don't know. I've got to go." I leaned over and impulsively kissed him on the cheek. He grinned and I jumped out of the car and headed up the driveway. I looked back and motioned for Mark to go. He waved and pulled away. Now I just had to hope nobody saw me.

*     *     *

So much for that. Dad was standing in the kitchen with his arms crossed, waiting for me.

"Who was that?" His words were sharp and quick.

"Mark gave me a ride home." I stood in the doorway to the mudroom, afraid to come any closer.

"Mark? The one from the play?"

"Yes." I readjusted the bag on my shoulder.

Dad looked up at the clock on the wall. "It's 4:30. It's a ten-minute drive from school. Where have you been?"

The truth and about a dozen lies popped into my head. I felt sick all of a sudden. I hated being in trouble. But I was trapped. I couldn't believe he chose this one day to come home early. But it sounded like he didn't see me kiss Mark. Good thing too, considering how mad he was about just riding in Mark's car.

"Just around."

"Specifics, Rebekah."

I hadn't seen him this mad since I got caught coming home in the wee hours of the morning after sneaking out to go to a party before Christmas, but if I told him the truth, he'd be furious.

"We just went for a drive. He offered me a ride home."

"It's not the ride home that's the problem, and you know it! What have you been doing for the last hour and a half?"

"Can we talk about this later? I have to get my homework done." I would have made a move for the stairs except he was completely blocking my path.

He didn't say a word. He just stared at me with a mixture of anger and, maybe, fear.

I dropped my head back and yelped in frustration. I looked back at him and said, "I didn't do anything wrong. Why does everything have to turn into some huge crisis?"

"If you were out with this boy alone, then you broke the rules. You know the rules."

"But we're just friends. I don't get why it's such a big deal."

"The point is, Beka, that you aren't supposed to be running around with people I don't know—especially if they're boys. If you want to date, then you have to do it right, by the rules."

"But we're not dating. He's not even allowed to date. We're just friends." My voice was way up, but I couldn't calm myself down. Too much was at stake.

"Friends or not, you broke the rules."

I shook my head and threw my bag on the floor. "This is ridiculous! Nobody has rules like this. Why don't you trust me?"

"Trusting you is one thing, and trusting him is another."

"Can I go?" I asked.

"Go. But we're not finished with this conversation." He stepped aside.

"Great." I knew he hated sarcasm. I walked past him, stomped up the stairs, and slammed the door to my room. But when I got there I collapsed on my bed in tears. Why was everything such a mess? I didn't know what to do. I felt panicky inside. Things had been going so well with my dad and I blew it. One drive to the Inlet and I had ruined everything. And the worst part was I didn't know how to fix it. How was I going to convince my dad I didn't do anything wrong when I knew that I shouldn't have gone? It would have been so easy to let Mark kiss me, to do exactly what my dad probably already thought. My stomach knotted up. Did he think I did something? Could he think that I would even . . . ? I didn't even want to think about it. But part of me thought I should have just let Mark do what he wanted. Then maybe it would be worth everything I had just lost.

I tried hard to concentrate on my homework, but I couldn't make my mind stay still. Nothing in my life seemed to make sense. I wandered into the bathroom and sat on the floor staring at the medicine cabinet for a while. It was only a little while ago that I had thought about swallowing a bottle of aspirin so that I could disappear. In my mind, I could still see the little pills spread across my blue bedspread. For months after my little bout in the hospital, Dad kept all the medicine locked up in his room, but over the last several weeks he stopped locking them up, and the bottles were now back where they used to be. I didn't even have to open the cabinet to know where the aspirin was—top shelf all the way to the right.

Disappearing just didn't sound bad at the moment. I had really thought that following God would make my life easier, but instead it seemed harder and more confusing. I not only had my own thoughts to deal with, but I was always trying to figure out what God thought about something too. And I didn't really know what God thought about anything. Even though I was reading the Bible every morning, it didn't seem to answer the millions of questions that regularly spun through my head.

Did I really want to die? Julie, my counselor, asked me about it every week, and I always told her no, but the thoughts did creep in every once in a while. Like the shadow of a tree falling across the carpet in a room, suddenly the thoughts would be there. The whispers that say, *It would be easier if I weren't here, Things just keep getting worse, and Would it really be so bad?* Unlike last time there was no panic in my heart. I was just aware of the shadow that lingered.

Eventually I got up and went and sat at my desk. I couldn't concentrate, but I didn't want my dad to find me in the bathroom staring at the medicine cabinet. I didn't want to have to explain anything.

It was after six when the knock finally came. Even though I was expecting it, I still jumped. I laid my pencil down next to my trig book and turned in my chair.

"Come in," I said.

The door opened and my dad walked in. He looked calmer but still very serious. I felt like throwing up.

He sat on my bed. "Are you ready to tell me where you were?"

"We were just driving around."

"Beka. I'm really disappointed. I thought I made myself clear about the rules."

"Yeah, the rules about dating and you having to meet the guy and all . . . that, but we never talked about having male friends. I'm not allowed to have male friends?"

"I don't know, Beka. You keep throwing me all these curve balls." He ran his hand through his hair and looked around my room. "You're growing up."

*Duh.* I didn't say it out loud. I was already in enough trouble. He sat for a few minutes. "Spending time alone with a guy constitutes dating as far as I'm concerned. The same rules apply."

"But, Dad . . ."

He held up a hand. "I don't want to hear it. You're grounded. And I don't want you seeing this Mark for the time being."

"What? That's not fair. You can't take away my friends."

"I'm doing this for you, really."

"Yeah, right," I muttered. I turned back to my desk, kicking the wall with my foot. I took a deep breath and turned back to him. "Why do you always overreact about everything?"

"I don't think I am." He frowned and drew his eyebrows together.

"You're totally overreacting. Why should I get grounded for doing nothing?"

"You broke the rules." His voice went up.

"I got in a car. Believe me, there are much worse things I could have done."

"What is that supposed to mean?"

"It means that I'm a good kid compared to most, and you treat me like I'm a delinquent."

"No, I don't."

"Yes, you do! I'm almost seventeen. You can't control me like I'm seven anymore. You don't treat Paul like this. You trust him to make decisions. Why can't you trust me?" Now the tears were dangerously close to the surface, but I didn't want to stop. He looked like he was weakening.

He turned away and took several breaths. I leaned on my desk and chewed on my pencil.

After a few minutes he looked back. "I've listened to you. I'm going to think about all this, and pray. But for now, you're still grounded."

I started to protest and then thought better of it. At least he was going to reconsider. I turned back to my trig book.

"We'll talk later," he said as he left the room.

I ignored him.

All the things I couldn't ask now went racing through my head. The guitar lessons, the prom. One stupid car ride ruined everything. I sucked in a deep breath. If I was going to get in trouble I might as well make it worthwhile. And I wasn't about to give up Mark.

*     *     *

I tossed and turned all night. I was mad and I wanted to get back at my dad, but I knew that God probably wouldn't be impressed with that. But why wasn't God talking to my dad about how unfair he was being? God knew what happened, even knew I had stopped Mark from kissing me. The more I thought about it though, the more I began to wonder what I would have done if we were actually dating. Would I stop him? Or was I simply trying to make a point that he needed to make up his mind what he was doing with me? Josh kept popping up in my thoughts too, but every time he did I'd think about how far away he was going. No, Josh wasn't going to be around. Mark was.

I was tired the next morning, but I took my time getting ready. I couldn't think of a way to see Mark over the weekend without lying. I knew Lori wouldn't cover for me, or even Nancy. Even though I wanted to see him, I didn't want to use my friends to do it. Twice I noticed my Bible lying on the floor before I went downstairs, but I didn't open it. I had read every morning for weeks, but I wasn't in the mood today.

\*     \*     \*

"What's going on?" Paul asked as soon as we had climbed in the car.

"Nothing." I opened my chemistry book and showed it to him. "I have a quiz today."

"No, I mean you and Dad. You were avoiding each other all morning."

"He's mad at me, and I think he's being insane." I filled him in on my ride home with Mark, leaving out the little trip to the beach.

"You should have known he'd be ticked," Paul said.

"He wouldn't have cared if you drove a girl home," I

argued. "It's a double standard. Besides, Mark and I are just friends."

"So how much trouble are you in?" he asked as he parked and climbed out of the car.

"Not sure yet."

We had already gone in different directions before I realized that Paul hadn't lectured me. I smiled. It was nice when he acted like a brother.

*     *     *

I filled Lori in on the situation at lunch. She didn't say anything for several minutes.

"It's Mark, right? You don't like him," I said.

"I don't know him. But if it's causing problems with your dad. . . . It might just be me, though. I'm so excited to have parents, I want to follow the rules. It's my way of showing them that I appreciate what they've done for me. I know most kids would think I'm some sort of a freak, but most kids don't know what it's like to have no one who cares about you either."

"You're not a freak," I said. I pushed some mushy peas around on my tray.

"Do you really like him?" she asked.

I thought about that. "Yes. He makes me feel special." I decided against mentioning how he was always trying to kiss or touch me. "I just want the chance to get to know him."

"What about Josh and the dance?" she asked.

"He's moving to Seattle, remember?"

"I know, but you already have permission to see him."

"For the dance. Josh hasn't asked me out, and he just wants to be friends anyway."

"Isn't that what Mark said too?"

"Yeah, but that's just out of necessity."

"I don't know. I'd still vote for Josh," she said. She drank the last of her juice and stood up to leave. She smiled sadly. "Can I do anything?"

I shook my head. There wasn't even anything I could do.

"Well, I'll talk to you later. Mom said she might be able to take us out shopping for dresses this weekend. What do you think?"

"Sounds great, but I might be grounded. I'll have to see."

She shrugged. "Well, let me know what happens."

I agreed, but I didn't have much hope. But when I was walking to journalism, I saw Mark headed right toward me. He smiled, and when he reached me he threw his arm around my shoulder and walked with me.

"Hey Beautiful. Where're you headed?"

"Journalism."

"Can you stay afterwards? I can start showing you some chords," he said.

"I want to, but I don't think I can. My dad saw me getting out of your car and . . . well, you know."

"You don't think he'll let you take lessons?"

"It's not the lessons, it's being with you, alone, that's the problem."

He smiled and raised his eyebrows at that. "He may have a point." When he said it he slipped his hand from my shoulders to my waist. I didn't push him away. More than one girl noticed in the hallway, and it gave me this weird sense of power. I wondered what the Public Display of Affection meant though.

"It's just you'd have to meet my dad and get the okay, even to be friends, which I think is stupid, but what am I supposed to do?"

"I'll meet your dad. Look, Beka, if it will make things better for you, I'll do whatever you want me to. Let him know I'm an upstanding kind of guy."

"I told him we're just friends." It felt so good to have his arm around me I was disappointed when we got to my class.

"And we are. Officially." We stopped and he moved me over to the wall. He played with a strand of my hair and curled it around his finger. "We'll think of something. Don't worry." He leaned in close, but he just winked and then walked down the hall. That's when I saw Gretchen standing directly across from me with an amused look on her face.

She walked toward me to go in the room, but stopped in the doorway for a second. "Well, well, Madison. I didn't know you had it in you." She went in, followed by Mai who glared at me, Theresa who ignored me, and then Liz. Liz smiled though.

"Hey," I said before Liz went inside. She came back in the hall after checking to see where Gretchen was.

"Can I ask you a question?" I thought since she had been nice even after I had turned them in, it was worth a shot.

"Sure." She folded her arms and leaned one shoulder against the wall.

"What's going on with Gretchen? I mean, she's talking to me again, but she hasn't said a word about the Snack Shack thing."

Liz shifted and stood up straight. "I don't know." I didn't believe her.

"Please? I have to know what's going on."

Liz was quiet for a minute and then lowered her voice. "I really don't know. She knows I don't blame you for doing what you did, so she doesn't tell me much— about you, that is. If I were you though, I'd be smart about it and watch your back." Liz turned and went in the room, and the bell rang loudly right above me. The halls were empty, but I didn't move. I so wanted to transfer schools and escape everything. Even having Mark's attention wasn't enough to keep me from worrying. Gretchen had way too much motive to get back at me, and entirely too much ammunition.

* * *

At dinner, Dad said we needed "to talk." So, after everything was cleaned up, we went into the family room and sat down.

"I've thought about what you said to me last night. And I do think we need to take a look at the rules."

I sat up a little straighter. Maybe this wouldn't be so bad.

"But you know you're not to be alone with boys I don't know. That rule is not going to change."

I stayed quiet and pressed my lips together.

"Originally I came upstairs to ground you for a month.

I couldn't believe it when I saw you climb out of the car. I really thought you were trying to earn my trust back."

"I am," I said.

"That's not how to do it. But I think we'll just keep it at two weeks."

Two weeks was better than a month. "Can I still go to the dance with Josh?"

He nodded slowly. "As long as you go with another couple."

"That's fine. After the two weeks, can Mark come over and meet you and get this all over with?"

"Are you saying you do want to date him?"

"Maybe." I shrugged my shoulder. "But I can't spend any time with him to find out if I do if you don't meet him."

"I know this must be hard."

I didn't think he had any clue at all. I doubted his parents turned dating into some huge ordeal. Why couldn't it just be simple and normal? Nothing in my life was ever simple and normal.

"I still need to get a dress though, and I can't wait two weeks. What about going to the mall this weekend with Lori and her mom?"

He was quiet for a minute and then nodded. "That's fine. Is that the way you want to do it? I could try to help . . ."

I lifted my hand. "No, it's a girl thing."

"Alright. We can talk about Mark after the two weeks. Is that fair?"

Livable maybe but not fair. I agreed and went upstairs to my room. It was going to be a long two weeks.

Except for the trip to the mall, I spent the next two weeks basically locked in my room. Dad had taken my phone away, which I thought was cruel and unusual punishment. It didn't make sense to me. If he wanted me to feel bad about what I did and follow the rules, then why did he always go out of his way to make me mad at him? It just made me want to be with Mark all the more, and I wasn't feeling overly concerned about the rules.

The worst part was that even though I didn't feel guilty about what I did, I was starting to feel guilty about God. I was avoiding my Bible. It was still lying on my floor, and I was stepping over it ten times a day, but

I never picked it up. Somehow, I knew if I picked it up, I was going to have to stop being mad at my dad. And I wasn't ready to yet.

I had gotten a beautiful dress though. It was a shimmering emerald green fitted dress with cap sleeves and a matching scarf. Lori had found a pale pink dress with ribbon trim along the hem and waist. It had taken us forever to find dresses that passed Megan's "flesh inspection," but it had still been fun.

Mark had changed his routes in school, because I was now running into him regularly, and more than one girl had shimmied up to me saying how lucky I was or asking how I had gotten Mark out of the convent. I never argued with them. I just let them believe we were a couple, especially since Mark acted like we were too. But then, the day before Josh's formal, I went and blew it again.

*       *       *

Mark had found me at my locker when school let out and asked me again about when we could get together outside of school.

I was crouched down swapping out my books at the bottom of my locker. "I was thinking, if it's okay with you, that I'll ask my dad about having you over next week. I just wanted to get my punishment and this dance over with."

"Dance? You mean the prom?" Mark asked.

I stopped moving, instantly realizing what I had said. I took a deep breath and stood up to face him.

"No, it's another dance I'm going to."

He folded his arms, and with his chin he urged me to continue.

"It's nothing. Josh asked me to go to his homeschool formal."

"And you're going?" He looked hurt, but I wasn't buying it.

"Yes, I'm going. We don't have some exclusive contract, Mr. Floyd. So until something changes . . ."

Mark said nothing, but I felt my heart drop into my stomach. I tried to smile at him. "Seriously Mark, it's just a dance. And Josh is moving to Seattle."

He stared at me.

"I'm just friends with him." I turned and put my hand on his arm. "Don't be mad. I should have told you about it."

"Yeah, that would have been nice. I gotta go." He turned and walked off, and I dropped my head back to stare at the ceiling. Just great.

*     *     *

I tried to put it out of my head, but it didn't work very well. I felt guilty, but there really wasn't a reason to. Mark and I weren't dating, and nothing was official. But if he did the same thing to me, I'd feel dreadful and would probably be just as mad. I didn't know what to do. I couldn't cancel going to the dance. Besides, I wanted to go. It sounded like fun and I wanted to see Josh.

On the way home, Paul asked me what was wrong, but since he didn't really approve of the Mark thing anyway, I didn't tell him anything. Dad caught me in the kitchen as I was piling up all my stuff to spend the night at Lori's. He looked sad.

"I know you're not happy with me, but I hope you have a good time tomorrow."

"Thanks." I opened up my bag to double-check that I had everything. I didn't look at him.

"Beka."

I looked up.

"Sure you don't want to have him pick you up here?" he asked.

"Dad. It's all arranged." I looked up. "Megan'll take pictures."

"Well, I understand." He put his hands in his pockets. "Well, have fun." He turned and left the room, and I leaned against the counter. I didn't want to feel sorry for him. I wanted to stay mad. He was making my life miserable with his rules. I zipped up my bag and threw it over my shoulder. I picked up the hanger draped with a red and black plastic bag that covered my dress, and I headed out the door. I wasn't going to let anything ruin this night.

*     *     *

"We could either pin up part of it or all of it." Megan had two handfuls of my hair, and I watched in the mirror as she twisted them up on my head. "What do you think?" she asked.

"I don't know. I always wear it down. Maybe we should put it up," I said.

"I agree," Lori said from across the room. She had set up another mirror on her nightstand and was sitting on the bed putting on her makeup. Megan had already piled most of her hair on her head, and some long strands that she had pulled from the mass of hair now curled gently around her face.

"Okay, here it goes." Megan pushed, pulled, and pinned my hair, trying to get it twisted at the back of my head. She used hairspray and bobby pins to tuck in the flyaway strands, and then pulled out some strands to hang out of the twist. She had to use a curling iron on my hair though; Lori's was naturally curly.

"There. What do you think?"

I used a hand mirror to get a look at the back. It looked really good. I smiled at her.

"Thanks."

"Oh." Megan jumped and splayed her hands out. "I forgot about the flowers." She ran out of the room and I turned and looked at Lori. Lori shrugged and went back to her face. I unzipped my bag and got out my makeup bag. I never used much makeup normally, just a bit of foundation to help mute my freckles, and a little mascara and lip gloss, but tonight was different.

Megan came back in digging in a large plastic bag. "Here they are." She pulled two bunches of small white fabric flowers from the bag and then tossed the bag on the bed. She unwrapped the flowers and then tucked some of them around my hair using more bobby pins to secure them. "Here Lori, let me do yours." Lori got up and sat next to me on the small bench I was sitting on and let Megan tuck the flowers in her hair too.

"You two look beautiful!" Megan clasped her hands over her mouth, and her eyes got glassy. Lori and I grinned. The dresses were perfect for us. My green one made my eyes sparkle, and Lori's pink one made her look like a perfect china doll.

"Can I pray for you guys?" Megan asked.

Lori and I nodded and bowed our heads. I tried to listen to Megan's prayer, but my head was swimming with so many other thoughts. Thoughts about my mom and how much she would have loved to be there. Thoughts about my dad, home tonight with Anna. And Mark, wondering if he hated me now. And Josh. I wondered what Josh would think of me after tonight. Maybe he would fall in love with me and decide he couldn't bear to go to Seattle and he'd transfer to . . . what was I thinking?

"Okay, let's get some pictures of the two of you before the boys get here." Megan went downstairs, and Lori and I grabbed our miniature handbags and followed her. Megan used her medium format camera to take our pictures. She had set up a white muslin backdrop across the back wall of their family room. Kari Lynn dressed up in a Cinderella costume and insisted on being in some of the pictures. But as time went on, my stomach started churning. It was my first real, honest-to-goodness date. I felt excited and backward all at the same time. Before my mom died, I wasn't allowed to date, and then she died and there weren't any prospects. I didn't know if it was because guys didn't know what to say to me or if there was something wrong with me. Even now, the "relationships" I had were more confusing than anything else. What would it be like? I was really, really glad that I was going with Lori and Brian. I would have been throwing up by now if I had been home with my dad.

Then the doorbell rang and I thought for a second I might be running to the bathroom after all.

Megan went to answer the door, and we heard her say, "Hi Brian. And you must be Josh. Come on in. I'd like to get a few pictures if you don't mind."

Josh came around the corner. Brian was probably there too, but I didn't notice anyone but Josh. He had a tux on and was carrying a small plastic box with a flower inside. His face lit up and he took a visible breath when he saw me, which instantly made my heart melt. All thoughts of Mark flitted out of my head. He walked toward me, never breaking eye contact, with the box in front of him. When he got close he breathed, "You look like an angel."

I had been smiling the whole time, so I just smiled wider. "I don't think angels wear green."

"You should." We stood looking at each other for what seemed like forever, and then somewhere in the distance I heard Megan's voice.

"Beka, Josh, you're next. Then I want to get pictures of all four of you."

"Shall we?" Josh offered me his elbow, and we went and stood in front of the muslin and got the pictures done. I felt like everything was going in slow motion. I couldn't stop smiling, and Lori looked at me more than once and raised her eyebrows at me.

Megan snapped just a couple more pictures, and soon we headed out the door. My dress had come with a matching wrap for my shoulders, and Josh helped me put it on. I thought he held his hands on my shoulders just a bit longer than necessary.

"Beka look!" Lori squealed. She pointed to the driveway where there was a long white limousine.

"It's only for the way there, but we thought it would be fun," Brian said.

We climbed in and the driver, Charles, drove us to the country club by way of the lake. It was beautiful, but all I could think about was the guy next to me. They all chatted during the drive, but I didn't have anything to add. When Charles pulled up in front of the clubhouse, he got out to open the door for us.

"You kids have fun, now. Be good," he said.

Josh offered me his elbow again but leaned down and whispered in my ear. "You okay?" he asked.

"Sure, why?"

"You're just quiet," he said.

"Just soaking it all in. That's all." I waited while Josh gave the tickets to two parents standing in the doorway. We walked into an elegant ballroom where one half was set up with tables and the other half was a dance floor. We were ushered to a table with four places, and before we had even gotten settled, our salads were served. Josh was on one side of me and Lori was on the other. This time, I tried to contribute to the conversation, but I tried to look around too. There were probably places for a hundred or so, and kids our age were being seated and served their meals the whole time. Then, as somebody finished, busboys would come and clear the table, whip off the tablecloth, and the table would disappear. I could hear soft music playing from the DJ stand on the opposite end of the ballroom.

During a break in the conversation, Josh leaned closer to me and asked, "So what do you think you want to do, Beka?"

"I'm sorry. Do?" I put my fork down and shifted toward him.

"Yeah. College, jobs. What do you want to do?"

"Oh, well . . ." I shrugged. "I guess I really don't know what I want to be when I grow up."

He laughed softly.

"Have you always wanted to be a doctor?" I asked. Deflecting questions was always a good tactic.

"Always," he said and nodded. "I was always getting hurt playing sports. I've broken bones, gotten stitches, needed X-rays. I guess somewhere along the way I decided that was what I wanted to do. Then God confirmed it when I got older."

I crinkled my nose. "Confirmed it?"

"Yeah, like someone else agreeing with what you think God is telling you."

I didn't want to seem like an idiot, but I didn't really understand.

He continued, "I've always wanted to be a doctor, but when I was fourteen I went on a mission trip with my family to Romania. A pastor I had never met before, and who didn't know my family, was introduced to us soon after we got there. When he shook my hand he said, 'You've got the hands of a physician, my boy.' I've never forgotten that. Anyhow, that's confirmation. Somebody else saw what God wanted to do with me, so I am sure that I am doing the right thing."

"Oh." I wiped my mouth as carefully as I could and set the napkin back down in my lap. "That's amazing." I didn't know what to think.

"So do you have any ideas?" he asked.

"Afraid not. I want to go to college, but I don't know what I'll study."

"No thoughts?"

I smiled. "Nope."

"Well, I'm sure God will show you when it's time." He stood up and held out his hand. "I think it's about time we had a dance." I put my hand in his and let him pull me out of my chair, but when he did, I got my heel caught in my hem and couldn't move my foot to steady myself. I fell headlong into his arms.

Whoa! I got you." Josh stood me upright and smiled.

"Thanks." I felt the fire in my cheeks.

"Now. How about that dance?" He took me by the arm and led me down to where many of the kids were already mingling. The tables were just about cleared, the music had gotten louder, and the lights were dimmer on that side of the room.

We all danced in a circle for a while until the music slowed down. Lori and Brian paired off, and Josh suddenly swept me into a circle. He held me the old-fashioned way with one hand on my back and the other hand holding mine.

He didn't say anything, just spun me slowly around the dance floor. I didn't even try to come up with a conversation topic. I would look around the dance floor and then he would catch my eye for a few moments, and then we'd start over again. I didn't even have to think much about the dancing because Josh knew exactly what he was doing.

"Where did you learn to dance?" I asked after a while.

He smiled. "I never thought it would come in handy. To tell you the truth, my mom made me. I hated it. But I do like this."

I took a deep breath and looked around. "It's smaller than I thought it would be."

"The network is pretty large, but not many of us are the right age for something like this. A lot of kids stop homeschooling when they get to high school."

"But you kept it up. How come?" We had slowed down so we could talk, but I felt like we were closer. I wondered if it was my imagination.

"So I could get a jump start on college. College and then medical school. It's going to take a long time. An extra year head start will be great."

"What kind of doctor do you want to be?"

"Now that," he leaned in, "is something I can't figure out. Not that I really have to. I'll have residencies and all of that to try out different things. But I like to have a plan. It's hard not knowing where God is taking you."

"Yeah, but at least you know something."

He looked at me and tilted his head to the side as if he was thinking. "God tells us His plan in His own way and in His own time. We just have to trust that we have a purpose, and God wants to get us there."

I thought about that. I remembered Lucy had been talking about a similar thing. But I didn't care so much about my whole life, or some big purpose. I just wanted to know where to apply to college, maybe what I should study. I still wasn't so sure that I mattered much in the big scheme of things. There just wasn't anything very special about me. I was a good student, but not the best. I wasn't very popular, and I certainly wasn't athletic like the rest of my family. I just really didn't fit anywhere. And if God did know where I fit, He wasn't talking, at least to me.

The music stopped and Josh took my hand to lead me off the dance floor. Lori walked toward us, smiling. "Come with me?" she asked.

"Excuse us," I said to Josh. Josh smiled and headed toward Brian, who was standing at a snack table.

Lori wrapped her arm around mine, and we walked down a long hallway to find the restrooms.

"So?" she asked.

"He's wonderful, smart, sweet, not to mention nice to look at. But he's moving to Seattle, Lori."

She screwed up her mouth. "I know."

"And you?"

She grinned. "Ohhhh, he's beyond words. I think I'm in love."

"What?" I stopped outside the restroom. We waited while a couple of other girls walked past us. "Are you serious?"

"Totally. And it's not that crazy if you think about it. Plenty of people marry their high school sweethearts."

"You hardly know this guy." I was so surprised. Lori was always so levelheaded, and she was acting like she had lost her mind.

"It so doesn't matter."

"How does he feel?"

She dropped her head and lowered her voice. "He said he can't imagine being away from me now that he's found me."

"He said that?"

She nodded and pushed the door into the bathroom. I took a few minutes to process that. I knew exactly what that stabbing feeling was in my gut. I really wanted to be happy for her. I went into the handicapped stall and leaned against the wall, trying not to squash my hair. It just wasn't fair. What was wrong with me? Mark was mad at me, Dad was mad at me, Gretchen was being bizarre, and Josh was leaving. I took several deep breaths and forced myself to remember Josh's face lighting up when he saw me in Lori's living room. I thought about his arms around me on the dance floor, and the warm feelings began to spread back through me. No, it wasn't as simple or easy as Lori and Brian, but I did feel special.

"Beka? Are you okay?" Lori asked quietly. I heard her tap on my door.

"Yeah. I'll be right out." I said.

I unlatched the door. Lori had leaned against the counter waiting for me. I half-smiled at her. "I'm happy for you," I said. Of all people, she deserved to have something wonderful happen to her.

She drew her eyebrows together. "What's wrong?" she asked.

I looked in the mirror and slowly spread fresh lip gloss across my lips and then twisted the cap back on. I took a deep breath. "I just wish he weren't moving. That's all."

"Do you really like him?"

"I really do. There's just something about him. I don't know." I leaned on the counter next to her. "There's just nothing I can do about it."

"Well, you can stop thinking about it and just enjoy yourself for starters." She folded her arms in front of her chest.

I smiled. "You are absolutely right. No sense in wasting a beautiful night in the bathroom, right?"

"Right." Lori laughed and we linked our arms as we walked out of the bathroom. I pushed Seattle out of my mind.

*  *  *

Josh and Brian were still by the snack table, and they looked up as we got closer. Those soft brown eyes were going to haunt me. He reached out his hand to me and gave me a gentle smile.

"I thought I had lost you," he whispered with a grin.

"You can't get rid of me that easily." I pushed his shoulder gently, and he caught my hand as I brought it back down.

"I wouldn't want to." He pulled me close and looked into my eyes.

I held my breath for a moment and then smiled. "I'm glad."

After another moment he led me back to the dance floor and wrapped his arms around my waist. I couldn't think of anything to say because I was trying to make sense of the emotions that swirled around in my chest. Is this what love feels like?

I took a deep breath and tried to relax, letting my racing thoughts move away for a while.

I wanted the night to last forever. To not go back to school or even home. To not worry about when Gretchen might strike or where I would apply to college. To dance around the floor with Josh for the rest of my life sounded like the most perfect thing I could imagine.

After countless songs, Josh leaned back to catch my eye. "Do you want to go sit for a while?"

I nodded and he held my hand as he led me toward a corner that had chairs set up. It was quieter there, and Josh sat down away from the other kids who were standing nearby. He let go of my hand to take off his jacket. Shivers went down my spine. What was a guy like that doing here with me?

"Are you having fun?" he asked.

"Oh, yes. This is great. I like how it's kind of low-key. Like me."

He gave a small laugh. "Me too. They have these every year, but I haven't been before."

"How come?"

He shrugged and leaned back in the chair. "Just haven't. I've had some girls ask me before, but I don't like that. I like to do the asking." He turned and looked at me. "Do you go to the dances at your school?"

"Sometimes. I went to a couple of homecomings with a group of friends. But that was before my mom died."

He watched me for a minute. "That must be hard."

"I have good days and bad days." I smiled. "She would have liked you."

"Well, that's good." He pulled at his black bow tie and shifted in the chair. "How're things between you and God?"

"I have good days and bad days." I shrugged. "I sometimes just don't know what I'm doing. Or what I'm supposed to do. I really thought giving my life to God would make things easier, or at least less confusing."

"And I take it, it's not."

"Not at all." I told him about Gretchen and the whole fire incident. I even told him about the witchcraft and how I finally stood up to her. I left out my stay at the hospital but told him about how she was acting now. "And I know she didn't just up and forgive me or anything like that, so I don't know what she's doing."

"Maybe she doesn't care about it."

"She has a record, she's on probation, she got kicked out of the play. No, she cares all right. I just don't know what she might do."

"You don't think she'd hurt you, do you?"

I considered it for a minute. "Not physically I don't think, but she could do some damage."

"Sounds like a lot to deal with. Can I pray for you?"

I nodded and he leaned forward and took my hands

in his. He prayed for a while, asking God to help me know how to respond, to give me help to protect me from any attacks. I found my thoughts drifting to his hands on mine and his voice, confident and strong. I felt safe with him. When he finished he looked up at me. "Will you let me know if I can do anything to help?"

"I'm not sure there is anything."

"Still. I'll do what I can. Until August anyway."

I didn't want to think about that. I looked down at his hands, strong and tanned, holding my smaller, freckled ones. I couldn't believe that we had been going to the same church for years and now, just as I was getting to know him, he was about to leave. If I had met him earlier, maybe things would have been different. It all just seemed so sad.

"There you are!" I looked up to see Lori and Brian walking over to us. Josh and I dropped hands and stood up. I almost laughed, more out of nervousness than amusement. We had been praying and I was blushing as if we had been caught doing something naughty. Lori gave me a smile though to let me know that she had seen the hand-holding.

"They're going to just play a couple more songs and then it's over," Brian said.

"Yeah, come on over so we can all dance," Lori said.

Josh picked up his jacket, slipped it back on, and held out his elbow for me. "Shall we?" he asked.

We went back over and danced until they turned on all the lights and began breaking down the dance floor. Brian and Josh had brought Brian's car over earlier to take us home. Josh and I climbed in the backseat. I was hoping that Josh would take my hand again or give me some sign, but he didn't. By the time we got to Lori's, my thoughts were swirling again. How did he feel about me? What was he thinking? Did he feel like I did? Brian pulled up into Lori's driveway. I had always thought that on my first date I would have that awkward moment at the front door wondering if he might kiss me. I didn't think Josh would try even if we had been alone. He was too much of a gentlemen. But I wanted him to. I couldn't help it. It would help me to know where I stood with him. And maybe how he felt. Because I was pretty sure Josh wouldn't kiss a girl that he didn't care deeply about.

Lori and Brian got out and stood in front of the car. They stood close, whispering back and forth to each other, and they were holding hands. I couldn't tell what they were saying, but neither one of them seemed to notice anything but each other. We sat there awkwardly for a minute. Then Josh climbed out and came around to open my door. I closed the door behind me and leaned my back on the car. Josh stood in front of me, shifting his weight back and forth slowly.

"I'm so glad you came with me. I had a great time," he said.

"Me too." I smiled at him, searching his eyes.

He stepped forward and I held my breath. Could he be? He reached down and took one of my hands and looked back at me. "You'll let me know if you need anything, right?"

"Sure."

We stood like that for a long moment. The world just seemed to stop moving, and my heart fluttered around inside of me. Then he stepped back and turned and pulled my hand to walk around the car and then up to the front door. Brian had climbed back in the car, and Lori was nowhere in sight, but the front door to her house was open.

I walked to the top of the steps, and Josh stayed a step or two below me. I had never looked down at him before.

He took a deep breath and smiled. "Good night, Beka."

I smiled back, biting back my disappointment. I should be happy, thrilled even, and yet I wanted to know what he was thinking. "Good night. Thank you."

He let go of my hand. "See you tomorrow."

I nodded and watched him walk back over to the car and climb into the front seat with Brian. I wished I could have heard what they would say to each other on the drive home. I walked to the door and went inside. Megan and Lori were sitting on the couch, and Lori was talking as Megan nodded. They looked up when I came in the room.

"Did you have a nice time?" Megan asked.

"Yes. It was wonderful. I'm going to go upstairs and change."

"I'll be up in a minute," Lori said.

I walked upstairs slowly and grabbed my pajamas from Lori's room. Then I locked myself in the bathroom and sat down against the door. I needed to gather my thoughts.

Eventually I got up and changed, but I felt numb. It was a wonderful night, but I couldn't stop thinking about how I didn't know any more than I did that morning. Except how much I really liked him. Maybe even more. What did love feel like anyway? Being with Mark had this thrill to it. It was different with Josh—it was more intense with Josh. But I wanted to be with both of them. I liked both of them. I scrubbed the makeup off my face and changed into my blue and yellow pajama bottoms and my butterfly T-shirt. I went into Lori's room where she was already changed and sitting on her bed.

She broke into a wide grin when she saw me. She patted the bed. "Sit. Talk."

I flopped onto the bed on my stomach, and Lori shifted so she could see me.

"You first. You and Brian looked . . . I don't know. Did he kiss you?" I asked.

She shook her head. "I knew we probably shouldn't, but I kinda wanted him to, ya know?"

I nodded.

"He's just amazing." She stopped and looked at me. "Look, I don't have to tell you. I don't mind if . . ."

"No, it's fine. I want to know. Maybe it'll even help me figure out what I'm feeling." I smiled at her.

She looked at me carefully for a minute then took a deep breath. "Okay, well, like I said, he's amazing." She spent the next thirty minutes telling me every detail she had learned about Brian. Some of them twice. She was positively giddy.

"What does Megan think? Is that what you guys were talking about?" I asked.

She got quiet for a minute and picked at her bedspread. "She wants me to be careful." Lori looked up. "And I understand that. But I just know. I don't know how I know, I just know."

"Know what?" I asked.

"That he's the one." She lay back on her pillows and wrapped her arms around her legs.

"Is that even possible? We're sixteen years old."

"Almost seventeen," she said. "And I'm not thinking about getting married now or anything crazy like that. I want to go to college and he's starting at Tech in the fall."

I shook my head. "That's a long time to wait."

"Well, if I'm right, then it will work out, and if I'm wrong, then, I guess I'm wrong."

She didn't think she was wrong, I could tell.

"So tell me about your night!" Lori sat forward and crossed her legs.

"It was really wonderful. That's all," I said. I sat up too and pulled a pillow into my lap.

"That's all? Come on! I saw you holding hands with him, and you guys were staring at each other half the night."

I gave her a half smile. "Duh. Do I need to say it again?"

"That doesn't mean anything. Do you like him?"

"Yes." I sighed. "But it's more realistic with Mark. Mark's not moving."

"Realistic? You can't analyze this one like you're choosing what clothes to wear. What's your heart tell you?"

I took a deep breath. "My heart's saying, 'Don't get hurt! Don't get hurt!'"

"What do you think God's saying?" she asked.

I groaned. "Not a clue. I guess I figured since Josh was moving away that was my answer. It's Mark. For now anyway."

"But what about later? If you don't think you could marry Mark, then someone's going to get hurt eventually."

"I told Mark about this dance though, so I'm not even sure he'll speak to me again."

"Oh, I'm pretty sure he'll speak to you again. I've seen the way he looks at you. But should you be with him? Is that what God wants?"

"That's the problem. I don't know what God wants, and as far as I can tell there aren't any Scriptures that say, 'You should or shouldn't be with Mark.'" I rolled onto my back and put the pillow over my face and screamed into it.

Lori lifted it off my face and shook her head at me. "Don't give up. It seems to me that's the most important thing for us to figure out, how to know what God is saying to us. Then we just have to do it."

"I wish He'd be more clear."

"Me too."

*　　　*　　　*

I didn't sleep very well because I couldn't get my mind to turn off. How was I supposed to hear from God? Did He really talk to people? I thought about the butterfly He had sent to me the night I decided to follow Him. It was a sign for sure, but it was more of a knowing than a voice or a direction. I needed to know, needed that push in some direction. I felt like I was in a boat in the middle of the ocean with no oar and no idea which way to go even if I had one. I felt like I needed to be rescued. Again. I wasn't sure how long I wanted to stay in the boat.

*　　　*　　　*

Josh appeared next to me right before Sunday school started the next morning. He quietly sat down next to me while I was chatting with Morgan. Morgan gave me a little grin before she turned back around.

I turned to Josh and smiled. "Hey there."

"Hey yourself. You should have worn that dress today. You looked great."

I laughed. "That would have been a bit much, don't you think?"

"I guess."

Our cabin leader from the retreat, Dana, stood up in front of the room. "Let's get started, guys." Everybody slowly took their seats. "We're starting a new series this week. I'm going to be sharing about God's purposes for you. I think a lot of you believe you might have a purpose, but you don't really know what it is or where you're really going."

I sat up straighter. God really was listening to me.

"Before we get started, though, I wanted to let you know that a group at Bragg County High, I think they're called the Young Believers, is going to be sponsoring a message about abstinence. This is a great chance to share with the public school kids about the power of purity and why some of you have made that commitment. They're going to have a speaker speak at an assembly not this Friday but next Friday at 1:00 P.M. How many of you go to Bragg County?"

I slipped my hand in the air along with about twenty other kids.

"Well, I don't know how many of you are part of this club, but they'd like some of you, even if you don't go to the school, to share why you have made the decision to be abstinent. And, if you don't want to share, they're also looking for kids who will just stand with them onstage as a show of support at the end of the program."

I shook my head. I had enough problems without giving the kids at my school more ammunition. That was the event Gretchen had volunteered me to cover for the paper, though. I was going to have to get working on it if it was coming up.

"Any volunteers?" Dana asked.

No one moved.

"Come on, guys. They're trying to show teens that being abstinent is not just about faith, but it's being smart too."

Still no one moved.

Dana put her hand on her hip. "Are you serious? No one is willing to stand up and say they are going to wait to have sex?"

A few snickers started around the room.

"That would be like inviting torture," one guy in the front of the room said.

"Not to mention the end of our social lives," another one said.

The room erupted in murmurs of agreement. Dana shook her head and shifted her hand to her other hip. Then Nancy stood up.

"I'll go. I don't go to school there, but I'll go to support them. I don't mind if people know how I feel." Nancy turned so she could see more people. "Think about it. We're not just standing up for abstinence or purity; we're standing up for Christ. We're either working with Him or against Him."

Slowly, three, then four, then about a quarter of the room stood up with Nancy. Josh leaned over and whispered, "That's Nancy for you," and then stood up. I didn't stand. I had to remain neutral. After all, I was covering the event as a journalist and Ms. Adams always said that to get the real story we had to suspend our preconceived notions. At least that's what I told myself.

"Well, good. I knew some of you would be willing." She handed out a sheet of paper to each person standing. "This is the information you'll need, where to be and all of that. The number for the president of the club, Heidi something or other, is on the bottom. She says you need to call her if you're willing to speak."

Once everybody got their paper and sat down, I shifted in my seat and leaned over to Josh. "Has Nancy always been so bold?" I asked.

He shook his head. "Nah. She used to be really shy about things."

"Really?" I couldn't imagine that. Nancy always struck me as so confident and sure of not only her faith but who she was. "What changed?"

He turned and looked at me. "You should ask her about it. I'm sure she'd tell you."

Dana began talking about purpose again, so I shifted my attention back to her. I really wanted to listen today. I thought there might be some clue or message for me in it.

She talked about how we were created by God, basic stuff, but what struck me was something she said about how everybody has a unique voice and nobody else sounds exactly like us. So when we speak to God, He knows immediately it is us, and He is ready and waiting to hear our voice. It felt right in my heart. Something in me had always wondered how millions of people could be praying at the same time and God hear all of us, especially some sixteen-year-old living in Bragg County. Did I really matter? Dana made it sound like I did. But could I count on it? Could I count on Him leading me where I should go?

*     *     *

"Are you coming to the meeting today?" Josh asked after Dana had dismissed us.

"The Haiti thing?" I let that process. A trip with Josh wouldn't be so bad. "Sure."

I found my dad and he told me he would wait for me, though he seemed kind of surprised I was going. Josh led me to a room with about twenty people in it. There was a mixture of adults and several teens. I noticed Dana was there, but I didn't really know anybody else. Josh sat down next to me.

It was a whirlwind meeting. They passed out papers, talked about the cost, and said that there would be some training sessions to learn about the culture and language. One of the papers had a schedule on it. I was overwhelmed by it all and decided it was just too much. I thought there was no way I could go. But the "team," as they called it, had apparently already raised some money, and they kept saying, "Don't let the money stop you if you think you should go." The trip would happen right after school let out, before it got too ghastly hot down in the tropics.

"It sounds like everybody else knew about this. It's too late for me, isn't it?" I asked Josh afterwards.

"Do you have a passport?" he asked.

I nodded.

"Well, that's the only thing that would take a while. The meetings will start next week. So, do you want to go?" He smiled.

"What about the money? I didn't have a clue about all that stuff you were talking about."

"I doubt it would be a problem. I'll help you."

"Well, I'll talk to my dad about it," I said.

"Great. I think it would be a great experience for you," he said. I wasn't sure if he meant that in a "big brother" kind of way or an "I care about you" kind of way. Either way, it would be cool to spend ten days with him.

*       *       *

When I got home the caller ID said that Mark had called, even though he hadn't left a message. All my questions from church and thoughts of Haiti and Josh flew out of my head. Dad asked me about the dance at lunch, but I was so anxious to get to my room that I barely heard him. Mark was talking to me!

I had gotten my phone back, so I flopped onto my bed and dialed his number, taking a deep breath to steady my voice as it rang.

Mark's mom answered, and a few moments later I heard his hello.

"Hi. It's Beka." *Did he know my voice? Should I have said that?*

"Hey Beautiful," he said.

That warmth spread through me like a wildfire. "I'm sorry Mark. I should have told you. But he asked me a while back and I wasn't sure where we were at and . . ."

"I need to see you. Can you get away today?" he interrupted.

"Umm. I don't know. Why? What's wrong?"

"I just want to know if you're still mine." He sounded breathy and serious.

"Yours? Mark. We've talked about this. You're not even allowed to date, and I don't have permission to date you."

"That's just details. Minor details."

"Not minor for me. I got grounded for two weeks just for getting a ride home with you. Remember?"

"Can't you think of something?" he asked.

I had an idea, but I didn't know if I should risk it. I wanted to see him. But I didn't want to get in any more trouble, and I knew my dad was watching. But would it really be so wrong?

"Why don't we just do this right and get the humiliation over with? I'll ask my dad if you can come over to talk with him."

"Fine. We'll do that. But can't I see you today? I'll meet your dad whenever you want, but just be with me today."

I pulled at the phone cord by my bed and wrapped it around my finger. "Okay. I have to take my sister out for her horseback-riding lesson today. She'll want to stay for a couple of hours. Do you want to meet me out there?"

He agreed and I gave him directions to the farm. Before the turn into River Bend Farm, there was a small park with picnic benches and a stream. I told him to meet me there.

After I hung up, I flopped back on my bed. I felt thrilled and special, but I also felt guilty. But I was going to talk to my dad about Mark as soon as I got the chance. No big deal if I spent the afternoon with him. Right?

"Thanks Beka," Anna shouted as she ran from the car toward the barn. I climbed out and checked my watch. Twenty minutes. I looked up and saw Gabby talking to Anna, and then Anna disappeared into the barn and Gabby headed straight for me. I closed the car door and took a deep breath. As she got closer, I saw that she was wearing her barn uniform: dirty jeans, white T-shirt, and a flannel shirt tied in a knot at her waist. Her hair was at least brushed and braided. I don't think I would have minded her at all if she weren't after my dad. I just wanted her to stay away. I knew somewhere inside that I shouldn't hate her. That I should probably even care about her. But I couldn't bring myself to do it. Julie's face popped into my thoughts. I'd have to get working on that before Gabby wormed her way in too far. I didn't even like the name Gabby.

She stopped in front of me. I was glad she didn't give me some big grin as if we were friends. She just asked, "Do you want to ride?"

"No. I think I'll just take a walk if that's okay," I said.

"Have at it." She pushed her hands into her pockets and rocked on her feet.

I scuffed my foot in the gravel and looked around at the split rail fences lining the paddocks.

"I guess I'll go then," I said. I moved away from the car and headed back down the road.

"Beka."

I turned around.

"Look. I know you don't like me. And I understand, but . . ."

"You understand? You understand what it's like to lose your mother and then have some woman show up chasing after your dad?"

"I'm not chasing your dad, Beka." She tried to sound reassuring, but I wasn't buying it.

I stared at her.

"I want us to be friends," she said. "What can I do to prove to you that you can trust me?"

"Stay away from my dad. That'd be a start." I walked away, and this time she didn't call after me. What nerve. I was fuming by the time I reached the small park. There were no cars there, so I went and sat on one of the picnic tables. Did she seriously think that I would ever consider being her friend?

*Love her.*

I pushed the thought away. God couldn't expect me to love her. The woman who wanted to replace my wonderful, perfect, beautiful mother. Anybody but her.

I glanced at my watch to try and distract myself. He was late. He had never been late, and he was so insistent about meeting. I jumped off the picnic table and went down by the creek. I sat down on the new spring grass on the bank and dug pebbles out of the dirt to throw in the water. I focused on a stick caught on the bank. *If I can dislodge that stick, You'll take Gabby away, but if I can't then I'll try to be nicer.* I threw the pebbles but wasn't getting anywhere, so I stood up and searched for some bigger rocks. I found several closer to the water and dug them out. I hit the stick with the second one, and it went spinning down the creek.

Love her.

*Please take her away.*

Love her.

I sat back down on the bank and buried my face in my arms, keeping my muddy hands away from me. Doesn't God understand?

I suddenly felt arms go around me and squeeze. He moved to the side and I just let myself fall onto his chest. I couldn't even cry. I didn't even know what I needed. Maybe all I needed was this.

"Sorry I'm late, Beautiful."

I turned and looked at him, his face close. "You're here now."

He reached over behind me and brought out a single

red rose. "I had to see you so I could give you this. You have to know by now how I feel. I'm in love with you."

I took the rose with my dirty hand, unable to speak.

He leaned in to kiss me, and before I knew how to react I felt his lips on mine. I let him for a moment, then pulled away. How can something feel right and wrong at the same time? That retreat turned everything I thought was okay into some bizarre swirling mess.

"My hands are dirty," I said.

Mark laughed. "It doesn't bother me."

I looked at the water. He was still sitting very close, his knee resting on my leg. Every nerve in my body felt like it was on alert.

"Should we walk?" I asked.

He stood up and I scooted down toward the water so that I could wash my hands off. I couldn't do it very well, but I dried them off on my jeans and climbed back up the bank. He laced his fingers through mine, and we walked into the woods.

We walked for a while on a small trail. He was behind me, which made holding hands impossible after we got into the trees. I moved branches aside, then he'd get real close and take them from me, and then we'd move back apart. I felt out of breath every time he came near me.

We caught a glimpse of the creek every once in a while, and then suddenly the trail spilled us into a meadow. I couldn't tell where we were exactly, but there were some wildflowers growing on the edge of the meadow that I couldn't resist.

"Hey, I brought you a flower," he said.

"I know." I pushed him playfully. "But a girl can never have too many flowers."

"Well, then." He pushed up his sleeves and began picking flowers.

"I like the orange ones. I wonder what kind these are."

Mark had moved ahead of me and was picking them one after another.

"Hey, I was just kidding," I told him.

He turned and walked toward me with a big bouquet of flowers and a grin on his face. He kept moving forward until the flowers were getting smushed between us. He leaned in and kissed me again. Just a short one, then he moved back.

Then over Mark's shoulder I saw Gabby sitting astride a huge chestnut horse, walking right toward us. I shivered.

"What's wrong?" Mark looked at me, then followed my gaze over his shoulder. He stepped to my side and moved his hand away from me. He cleared his throat.

Gabby stopped her horse in front of us.

"Beka? What are you doing?" she asked.

"Nothing. Mark's just a friend from school," I said.

Mark smiled. "Hi."

"Hi," she said, without looking at Mark. "Does your dad know about this?" she asked me.

"Not exactly." I suddenly wished I had been a lot nicer to her.

She dismounted and let go of the reins. The horse moved away and began to nibble at the grass around the wildflowers.

Anna appeared from around the trees riding Wind

Dancer. She pulled the reins and stopped her horse when she reached us.

"Who's that?" Anna asked.

"Ummm. A friend from school. His name is Mark," I said. Mark moved away from me and walked toward Anna.

"That's a pretty nice horse you've got there," he said to Anna. He patted Wind Dancer on the neck.

"Thanks," she said. She looked around at us all, bewildered.

"Anna, why don't you head back to the barn," Gabby said.

Anna pushed out her bottom lip, dropped the reins, and folded her arms. "But I'm not done practicing. You said we could canter today."

Gabby looked from Anna to me and then back to Anna. "We will. I promise. Why don't you ride out there and practice your turns for a little bit. I need to talk to your sister."

Anna looked at us for a minute but then picked up the reins and walked Wind Dancer out to the meadow where Gabby had pointed. When she was too far away to hear, Gabby turned back to me.

"Look," I said. "We were just talking. Don't say anything to my dad, okay?"

"You weren't just talking."

"Mostly talking."

Mark didn't seem fazed at all. "Gabby is it? You can understand, can't you? We don't get much time to see each other at school."

"But you two planned this."

"It won't happen again," I said. "We just haven't had a chance to talk to Dad about it. Don't say anything. Please?"

"Beka. This isn't fair. You're putting me in a terrible position. You'll feel betrayed if I tell, but your dad will feel betrayed if I don't."

"But he won't find out."

Gabby lifted her arm and gestured to where Anna was riding. "What about her? You can't ask her to lie for you."

"I can handle her. She won't have to lie. She just needs to not say anything."

Gabby shook her head and folded her arms. "This isn't right, Beka."

"Please. I'm begging you. It's not going to happen again."

Gabby looked at me as if she was considering it. I chewed on my lower lip and held my breath. I took a glance at Mark and he winked at me. I would have laughed if I didn't feel so sick to my stomach.

"I won't say anything today. I think you should be the one to tell him anyway."

I looked at Mark. There was no way I could tell my dad.

"Thanks," I said. "I really appreciate it."

"I'll give you a week, Beka. You need to tell him by Saturday. Or I will."

I scowled at her. "That's not fair."

"It's more than fair. Now you," she pointed at Mark, "go back to wherever you came from. Beka, the barn is that way. You can wait for Anna there."

Mark and I looked at each other, but Gabby didn't

turn to leave. Mark reached out and held the bouquet of flowers out for me to take. "We'll talk later," he said. He disappeared back through the woods, and still Gabby hadn't moved.

"He's cute," she said.

"Like it matters. My dad's never gonna let me see him thanks to you." I walked past her to where she pointed.

"Beka, I said you could trust me. I won't say anything."

I whirled back around. "You might as well go ahead and tell him if you're going to make me do it anyway. I don't want him to know at all. How can I trust you if you're going to rat me out the first chance you get?" I turned and ran toward the barn with the flowers in my hand, crying. My life as I knew it was over.

\*       \*       \*

I found a small tack room that had some benches in it and collapsed onto one of them. I was exhausted inside and out. I laid the flowers in my lap and touched the petals and leaves, thinking about Mark smiling at me. His kisses. There was no way I could tell my dad. He would flip and never let me see Mark again. He would never understand.

I heard voices in the barn, and a few minutes later Gabby came into the room with two bridles on her arm. She hung them up carefully and then turned around to look at me.

"I still don't think this is right, and I still think you should tell your dad, but . . ."

I sat up straight and clutched my flowers.

"But I won't say anything. You're old enough to make your own decisions. Mind you, I think it's a bad one. And I don't want to be put in this spot again."

I shook my head. "Oh, I wouldn't, I won't. Thank you. Thank you so much." I relaxed back against the seat. Maybe Gabby wasn't so bad.

But Anna could still be a problem.

As soon as she climbed in the front seat Anna said, "Is that your boyfriend, Beka?"

"He's not my boyfriend, Anna. He's just a friend from school."

"But you have flowers," she sang.

"We're good friends," I said.

Anna leaned back on the seat and looked out the window. Would she even bring it up to our dad? I weighed my options.

"Anna, I'd rather you not mention Mark to Dad if that's all right," I said.

"How come?"

I shrugged. "Well, because Dad's going to meet Mark real soon. It's kind of like a surprise."

She crinkled her nose. "Why is it a surprise?"

"It just is, so don't say anything, okay?"

"Okay." She looked back at the window, and I took a deep breath. So far so good.

*　　　*　　　*

Dad went down to his workshop after dinner, and after I had finished the dishes, I followed him down. Paul was out with friends but Lucy and Anna, who had talked only about her riding at dinner, were watching a movie in the family room.

"Hey Butterfly," he said when I came down the stairs. I sat near the bottom of the stairs and watched him sanding a piece of wood. "Do you need to talk?" He kept sanding but turned to sit on an old metal stool so he could see me. The sound of the sanding sent shivers through me.

"I guess so."

He stopped sanding and laid the piece of wood and the sandpaper on the workbench. I looked down at my socks.

"Well, it's kind of about this dating thing." I glanced up. His expression hadn't changed, but he gestured slightly for me to continue. "Well, I guess I need to have you meet Mark to see if it's okay if we date." I looked back at my shoes, but I heard the stool creak as he shifted his weight.

"How about next Sunday after church? He can come over to lunch."

"With everybody here? I don't want to get into a big family thing. I just need you to meet him, right?"

"Okay, then after lunch."

"That's better." I started to get up.

"Beka, wait. I need you to help me understand what's going on. I thought you were more interested in Josh. What's going on with Mark?"

"Josh is moving away, Dad. He's nice but he's leaving. I'd like to date someone who'll actually be in this state."

"I can understand that. But dating isn't just some fun activity to do on the weekends; it's a process we use to choose the person we're supposed to be with."

"I don't want to get married. I just want you to let me date."

"I know. But dating is risky. You could get hurt. I don't want you to get hurt. If I had my way we wouldn't even be having this conversation."

"I'm almost seventeen. Lots of kids started dating a long time ago."

"I know. But God has an opinion about who you spend your time with, and who you date, and all of those things. Do you think God wants you to date Mark, or Josh, or anybody at all right now?"

"I don't know. It doesn't matter what I think anyway."

"It does matter. It just sounds like Mark is more convenient. That's not a good thing to base your decisions on."

"I just want to date. That's all. Why does this have to be some big complicated thing?"

"It doesn't. Look, I'll talk to Mark next week. We'll see."

I called Mark when I got to my room and asked him if he could come over. He agreed, but I didn't feel like talking. I changed into my pajamas. Home and ready for bed at eight o'clock. How pathetic was that? How could my heart be going in two different directions? And what did God think about it all? I hadn't even really asked. Mostly because how would I know anyway? My heart was so jumbled up I couldn't even sort out my own emotions. How was I supposed to know what God thought?

I picked my Bible up off the floor and looked at it. Was the answer really in there? I lay on my stomach on the bed and flipped it open. Things didn't seem like such a mess when I was reading it every morning. Dana had mentioned Esther the week before at church, so I looked for that. I had to check the Table of Contents to get a page number, and I began to read, "This is what happened during the time of Xerxes . . ."

*       *       *

I felt better when I woke up. I didn't have any answers, but the story of Esther was interesting. I knew I was supposed to apply the Scriptures to my own life, but I didn't know how it related to me exactly. I thought of the king as my dad who I was supposed to get favor from, and Gabby was Haman who could turn against me at any moment.

*       *       *

I was so busy worrying about my dad talking to Mark that the week passed by in a blur. I did read the Bible every morning, but if I was totally honest, I kept looking for hints about Mark and Josh and what direction to go. Every day in the hallway, Mark gave me some reason to smile, and if my dad liked him there was the possibility of a real date. More and more I felt like the answer was obvious, but when Sunday finally came, it was Josh who was on my mind.

We were all running a little late for church, so I hardly even noticed Anna arguing with my dad until I heard my name.

"What did you just say?" he asked.

Anna stomped her foot. "Beka got to bring a friend out to Gabby's, so why can't I?"

"What friend?" He looked over at me as I hovered by the kitchen table.

I froze.

"That boy. Matt or something. He got to come out there. I just want to show Jenny my new horse," Anna pleaded.

Dad straightened up to his full height and folded his arms across his chest. His face looked dark and angry.

Anna must have realized something was wrong because she looked between us for a minute. "Did I ruin the surprise?" she asked.

"Anna, get your things and go wait in the car. We'll talk about this later."

Anna disappeared and Paul and Lucy wandered through, and still he hadn't spoken to me. And I couldn't even begin to form a word.

"Start explaining." The words came out hard and quick.

What was I supposed to say?

"We're gonna be late." I shifted and moved away from him a little.

"Go get in the car," he said.

I grabbed my Bible from the kitchen table and ran past him. When I climbed into the car everybody asked me what was wrong all at once. I slumped into my seat and wished I could just disappear.

*       *       *

Church was dreadful. I couldn't sing, and when Josh sat next to me at Sunday school again, I couldn't stir up even a speck of joy about it. I snuck a peek at him every once in a while. If he weren't leaving, would things be different? I felt like I was pushing him away just because of his move.

"Are you okay?" he whispered at one point.

I just shook my head.

"Do you want to talk about it?"

I shook my head again.

I never even heard what Dana was saying about purpose. And as it neared the end of the class, I got more and more frantic inside. What was he going to do? I got this image of me being locked in my room until graduation. But even worse was that I knew he wouldn't ever trust me again. The look in his eyes bothered me more than if he had yelled and screamed at me about it.

The car ride home was deathly silent. Not even Anna

said anything. When we pulled into the driveway, Dad didn't shut off the car.

"Beka, you stay. Everybody else go on inside. Paul, can you see that they get lunch?"

"Sure," Paul said. They all climbed out. I was in the last row of seats, but I didn't move up. He pulled out of the driveway again and drove to a small Mexican restaurant. I followed him inside and sat across from him in the booth, keeping my head down. At least it was a public place.

The waitress came and took my dad's order, but when she got to me I just ordered a glass of water. When she left, Dad leaned back against the blue cushion.

"You ready to explain yourself?"

"We were just talking," I said. I pulled the sugar holder over and began to arrange all of the little sugar packets.

"Not the point," he said.

I looked up for a second and then back down. I moved the blue packets together.

"We had a conversation about this just a few weeks ago."

The realization hit me that Mark was supposed to come over at two o'clock. I looked down at my watch.

"We'll be back in time. Believe me, I am going to have a conversation with this boy."

I closed my eyes and leaned back. I wanted to curl into a little ball and hide in the corner of the seat.

"How many times have you seen him without permission?" he asked.

I opened my eyes. "He goes to my school. I see him every day."

"That's not what I mean. You obviously went for a drive with him a few weeks ago, and now this. Is there anything else I should know about?" My mind flashed to the trip to the mountains we took several months ago, but I wasn't going to add that to the fire.

I shrugged. "We're not doing anything wrong. We just wanted to talk."

"Not the point." He raised his voice just a bit. "You do not have my permission to see this boy. Period."

I clammed up. There was no way to defend myself, and he wasn't listening. I was just going to make things worse. We left the restaurant and got home in time to see Mark pull in the driveway.

He climbed out and grinned at me. Dad noticed and didn't seem happy. I wanted to warn Mark, but I knew I wouldn't get to talk to him alone. But Mark noticed that something was wrong, so he dropped the grin and held out his hand to my father.

"Hello again, Mr. Madison."

"Mark."

They shook and my dad led us through the kitchen, where Dad introduced Mark to everybody, and then into the family room.

We settled down apart from each other. I was impressed with Mark's ability to adapt to the situation. It's like he knew even without being told. I folded my legs and leaned on the arm of the couch.

Dad started off asking about Mark and his family. Mark answered everything politely. I just watched. It wasn't as bad as I thought it would be. Then Dad shifted to our little escapade the day before. My heart began to thump, but Mark didn't even seem flustered.

"Yes, sir. We went for a walk out there. I'm sorry if that was a problem. It won't happen again."

Dad eyed him for a minute. "Beka assured me it wouldn't happen after you two went driving after school. But it did."

"Well, sir. That's why I'm here I guess. I mean, we want to do things right."

"What do you want to do exactly?" Dad asked.

"Get to know each other, sir." Mark never flinched, while I had to force myself to not cringe.

"And your parents? How do they feel about dating?"

"Well, they'd prefer me to not get too serious. But they've given me permission to go to the prom, and I'd like to take Beka."

I blushed. I really didn't want to be in the room. But I didn't want it happening without knowing what was happening either.

Dad leaned back in his chair and looked at both of us. Mark looked at me for the first time since we came in the room. He didn't grin, but he looked at me with this "It'll be fine" look. I wasn't so sure.

"The problem is, I don't like the way this started. I'm uncomfortable with the fact that you've already been spending time alone together. I'm inclined to wait until the fall. If you still want to see each other then, maybe we can look at it again."

"But Dad . . ." I protested. He lifted a hand to stop me.

"Sir, I assure you, it won't happen again." Mark said.

"Son, to be honest, I don't know if I can trust either of you at this point. Beka, you've got some trust to earn back before I'm willing to give this my okay."

The tears sprung in my eyes before I could stop them. "So you're not going to let me go to the prom? How could you do that?" I held back the sobs that hovered in my throat. Mark didn't need to see me have a meltdown.

Dad looked at me for a minute. "When is it?" he asked.

"Three weeks," I said.

Dad tightened his lips and furrowed his brow. I held my breath.

"Since it's the prom, I think that would be okay for one night."

I sighed in relief.

"As long as there aren't any problems between now and then," he added.

It didn't even dawn on me until after I had said good-bye to Mark in the driveway that Dad had just nixed the idea of seeing Mark regularly. I stood in the driveway watching him leave. I'm sure my dad probably thought I'd want to earn back his trust, and I would want to make sure I did everything right.

But as I watched the little black car disappear, all I could think about was seeing him again. And I didn't want to wait for prom night.

Before breakfast was even over
the next morning, I already had a plan. The next night
Paul and Lucy were going to go to youth group after
their practices, Anna was having dinner at a friend's
house, and Dad had a late meeting. Perfect.

"I really need to go buy a few things for school and
go to the library. Can I do it after school tomorrow?"

Dad looked at me. I hated that he couldn't trust me,
but felt like there was nothing I could do about it either.
"So you're going to the store and the library? What time
will you be back?"

"Well, since everybody'll be gone I'll just grab some

dinner and finish my homework at the library if that's okay."

"Beka, you're grounded, remember?"

"It's not like I'm going to a party."

"Alright, well I want you back here by seven. Got it?"

"Can it be eight? I'd like to finish my report."

He looked at me as if he was trying to figure out what I was up to. I went and rinsed my bowl and put it in the dishwasher before he answered.

"Alright, eight. But don't blow it, Beka. I mean it."

I didn't respond, but I was grinning inside.

*       *       *

When I saw Mark, I told him that I had the whole afternoon the next day. He took my hand and slid his arm around me, putting my arm behind my back, and pulling me close.

"Then where should we meet?"

"Why don't you come to the library around four? That'll give me time to run to the store and make some copies. My report's already done, but my car should be there."

"Sneaky little thing, aren't you?" He laced and unlaced his fingers in mine behind my back.

I frowned. "I wouldn't have to be if he would just be reasonable."

"But we were naughty." His face was close, and I could smell the peppermint on his breath.

"Hmmm. Depends on your definition of naughty."

He kissed me on my nose and let me go. "Later,

Beautiful." He left me feeling flustered and out of breath. A second later Lori appeared at my side. She didn't look happy.

"I guess it went well with your father yesterday," she said.

"Not exactly. He'll let me go to the prom with Mark, but we can't go out. He said he might reconsider in the fall."

"Then what was that?"

"What?" I crouched down to get my books.

"Well, you guys looked pretty . . ."

"Well, just because we can't date doesn't mean that I'm not going to see him. Dad's not being fair."

Lori leaned back and put her head against the locker. "Beka. Are you seriously going to do this behind his back?"

"I'm not doing anything. I'm just spending time with a friend." I closed my locker a little harder than usual.

Lori shook her head. "I don't know, Beka. It's not right."

"Maybe not, but he should have just let me see him. He can't control my whole life, and he can't control my feelings."

"He's your dad. Remember the whole 'children obey your parents' thing?"

"But I'm not a child anymore. He wouldn't even discuss it. He's scared because I'm growing up and he can't handle it. That's his problem, not mine." I started walking down the hallway and Lori followed. She was silent for a moment, so I looked back to see if I could see what she was thinking.

Lori smiled sympathetically. "Would it be different if your mom were around?"

I looked away from her and down the hallway, thronged with kids laughing and talking. "I don't know. Maybe, but maybe not."

"Will he reconsider?"

"Not anytime soon. Right now I'm grounded because I saw Mark out at Gabby's farm on Saturday. He says I have to earn back his trust."

"How do you do that?" she asked.

"I don't know."

\*       \*       \*

I sat in the main foyer after school on a bench waiting to meet with Heidi about the Young Believers Club and their "Wisdom Says Wait" program. I already had my questions ready, and I had brought my camera to take her picture.

She came right on time. I had talked to her on the phone the night before to set up the interview, but she looked totally different than I thought she would. I was expecting some demure little girl wearing a lace shirt and jumper, and instead a tall, striking girl with her long hair dyed red and a tiny diamond stud in her nose walked up to me. She was wearing a shirt with a tie at the waist layered over the top of a long-sleeved shirt that was tucked into a pair of low cut jeans with a jeweled belt. I was amazed that she could look so stylish and modest at the same time.

"You must be Beka. I'm Heidi." She sat down next to me and handed me some papers she was carrying.

"These kind of explain what we're trying to do with our campaign. I'm so glad that you're going to cover it. Gretchen told me that you're a Christian too."

"Gretchen?"

"Yeah, we're on the cheerleading squad together."

That's where I had seen her. I really should work harder on my "preconceived notions."

"Oh, well. Yes, but I have to just tell the story for the paper."

"That's fine. I'm just glad you'll understand where we're coming from."

Heidi spent about an hour answering questions and explaining what they were teaching. She invited me to come to one of the health classes they were presenting in so I could see how they did the program.

"Did you all come up with this idea?"

Heidi nodded. "Our club has about fifteen members, and we wanted to do something in this area for a while. We've been planning this all year."

I snapped Heidi's picture and got their schedule for the week so that I could drop in on one of their presentations. When I left I couldn't shake some of the things she had said. But it was what she didn't say that stuck with me even longer. It was that same conviction I saw in Nancy and Paul and Josh. That total commitment to what they believed. Why couldn't I get there? What was wrong with me?

\*     \*     \*

After school on Tuesday I flew out to Wal-Mart to buy some notebooks and some hair products. Then I raced over to the library and copied several articles from some magazines about the state election. I had already finished my report, but it would be good to cover my tracks. At four o'clock I was standing in the foyer of the library, and a few minutes later Mark came in.

"Ready, Beautiful?"

I smiled and let him take my hand. A pang of guilt shot through me, but I pushed it aside. I left my car parked right in front and we climbed into his car. He turned onto the highway and headed toward Bonfire Beach. I pressed the button to roll the window down and lay back in the seat. It was a beautiful spring day. And I had Mark's undivided attention.

When we got to the beach, he parked right up front and we climbed over the logs. I slipped off my shoes and carried them in one hand, and he took the other as we walked a bit down the beach. We talked a little about our Sunday meeting with my dad, but Mark didn't seem worried.

"He'll come around," he said.

"Maybe."

We looped back around, and Mark had me sit and wait by the bonfire pit. I watched him open the hatchback of his car and pull out a big picnic basket. He walked over with a grin on his face.

"You made dinner?" I asked.

"Mom helped, I admit. I probably would have thrown it all into a brown bag, to be honest."

I helped him unpack the sandwiches and sodas. "So your mom knows about this?" I asked.

"Yeah. She was fine with it. She likes you. Of course, I told her we were just friends."

I looked at him.

"But you know I don't just want to be your friend," he said.

"So why'd you tell her that?"

"So she wouldn't worry. Besides, she has nothing to worry about, right?"

"Is she worried about you . . . you know . . ."

"Having sex again? Yes, that and me getting too involved with you."

"So how come she agreed?" I pressed.

"Because I promised her I'd be careful with you."

I looked around the deserted beach and shivered. A moment ago I had felt warm and fuzzy inside, and now I felt chilled. I felt so young and immature. I had never really thought I'd ever have a boyfriend, so I never really thought much about what I'd do with one. I had imagined walks on the beach and other such stuff, but the physical part had me a little spooked. What did purity really mean? I wasn't even sure what I believed. And figuring it out seemed really important all of a sudden. Mark was experienced. That in itself made me nervous. He seemed so confident when he kissed me and held me close. Not a speck of concern. But would he be content to stick with kisses?

After we ate, we stretched out on the sand with our heads propped up on the small blanket Mark had brought from his car. He scooted closer and turned over on his side and rested his head on his elbow. With his other hand he traced small circles with his finger over my stomach. Slowly he moved the circles lower until he caught the edge of my shirt, and I felt his finger circling my skin. I sat up.

He sat up too. "What's wrong?" he asked.

"Nothing. I'm fine. It's just getting late."

He glanced at his watch and lay back on the sand. "It's early. You said you didn't have to get back to the library until seven thirty."

I pulled my knees up and wrapped my arms around them. I didn't know what to do. I was in over my head, and I knew it.

I stood up and walked down to the water. My shoes were still near the picnic basket, so I waded into the water just a little bit. The water was cold, but it felt good. Mark came up behind me and wrapped his arms around me. His hands were on my stomach, under my shirt, and I could feel his thumbs caressing my skin.

He pulled me close and whispered in my ear, "I love you."

I let the words spin through my head for a moment. Then I broke free from him and stepped sideways. I used my hand to brush the top of the water and spray his face.

"Hey!" he yelled. He wiped his face and reached out to grab me, but I darted just out of reach and sprayed him again.

He let his hand hit the water, and I felt the cold water hit my face. I ran back up on the beach with him chasing me at full speed. I was no match for him. He tackled me, and we tumbled onto the sand. When we came to a stop, he was on top of me. Before I could move, he kissed me full on the lips. I wiggled free and sat up.

That's when I saw Gretchen's Jeep parked right next to Mark's car in the parking lot. Mark leaned back on his heels, and we both watched it back out then pull away. He looked at me and shook his head. "Who was that?"

"It was Gretchen," I said. I stood up and started brushing myself off. "Can you take me back to the library?"

"It's only six thirty." He looked disappointed.

"I know." I reached over and brushed some sand from his shoulders. "But I need to do something."

He frowned, but he walked over to the picnic stuff and began gathering it up.

I followed him and gathered the trash.

"I'm not going to have sex with you." I forced the words from my mouth.

Mark turned and looked at me. "I didn't expect you to."

"What exactly do you expect?" I straightened up.

He stood up too and turned to face me. "What do you mean?"

"Well, what do you expect to be able to do?"

"I don't know. I was just following you."

"So you'll do whatever I let you do?" I asked. I let the words come out before I censored them.

"No. I guess. But I've learned my lesson about being careful."

"I'm not talking about being careful. What do you think is right? What does God think about it?"

Mark shook his head. "You're thinking too much." He bent back down to pick up the soda bottles.

"Mark, we need to talk about this. You can't just leave it all up to me to stop you. What if I mess up? Then we'll both be in trouble."

Mark reached over and took the trash from my hands and walked it over to the trash can nearby. He closed the basket, picked it up, and grabbed the blanket. "Let's just see what happens. We'll take it slow."

"But we can't do that, because it really could happen. I never thought it could until today, but here we were. I may not be strong enough to say no. I like it when you hold me and kiss me."

He moved forward with a smile.

"No. I like it too much is what I'm saying. That scares me."

"So we won't. No big deal."

"Won't have sex or won't do other stuff?"

"I don't know. Whatever you want," he said. He walked toward the car and opened the hatchback.

"But what do you think? Really?"

"I really don't think this is such a big deal. We'll just let God lead us and see what happens."

"I don't think we're going to hear God in the middle of some moment. That's why we have to talk about this now." Was it me saying these things?

"But you stopped me today. Several times," he said.

"Barely," I muttered. I climbed in the car after brushing off the last of the sand.

"I like you Mark. I really do. But I just don't think I'm strong enough."

He started the car and backed out of our spot. "Why do you think you have to be strong?" he asked.

"Because you keep pushing."

Anger flashed in his eyes. "Pushing? I haven't . . ."

"I just mean that I feel like I'm the one who has to stop you. And I don't necessarily want you to stop."

He shook his head. "You've lost me. What are you trying to say?" he asked.

I couldn't believe it when the thought went through my head. "I think maybe my dad was right."

# CHAPTER 16

Becoming Beka    BECOMING BEKA

**What is that** supposed to mean?"
Mark asked.

I leaned back on the seat and looked over at him. He glanced between the road and me with a hurt expression on his face.

"I'm sorry, Mark. I really am. But maybe we should cool things off for a while. Wait until I have permission to see you."

I watched him tighten his grip on the steering wheel. "Beka. I'm not going to make you do anything you don't want to do. I'm not that kind of guy."

"I know you're not. It's not you I'm worried about. It's me. I'm afraid I'll do something I'll regret."

He didn't respond.

"It's not you Mark, I promise. I do want to be with you but . . . I'm trying to figure out this stuff with God, and I just feel I need to get that sorted out before I get in too deep with you. You know what I mean?"

"Are you breaking up with me?" he asked.

"No. I mean, how can I break up with you when we're not really going out?"

"A technicality," he said.

"I want to be with you. I just need some time to sort some stuff out."

"Fine." His voice had a hard edge to it. I turned and looked out the window. I couldn't believe I had started the conversation or where it had ended up.

He pulled into the library parking lot and put the car in park.

"Are you mad?" I asked.

He turned and looked at me, his eyes a little softer than they were before. "I don't know what to think. I thought we were having a great day, and then you hit me with all of this."

"I'm sorry. Just give me some time. Please?"

"What about prom?" he asked.

I took a deep breath. "I don't know. I mean . . ."

"Yes or no, Beka."

I twirled the ring on my pinky finger round and round.

"No. But it's not what you think. I don't think I'll be allowed to go with you."

"Your dad said we could."

"Yeah, but I haven't told him about today."

"Why would you do that?"

"Because I have to." I climbed out of the car and shut the door. The engine revved, and I watched him tear out of the parking lot. I felt like I was watching my one and only chance at a boyfriend disappear. And it was all my fault.

I drove straight over to Lori's house. I wished I had a cell phone to call and see if it was okay, but I didn't. When I knocked on the door, Megan answered.

She smiled and then frowned. "Are you okay, Beka?"

I burst into tears. She ushered me into the house and took me downstairs into their family room. Lori appeared and followed us down. I didn't even notice if Lori's dad was there.

Megan kept handing me tissues, and they both sat and waited until I had calmed down.

"I don't even know why I did it," I cried.

"Did what?" Megan asked.

I told them about the trip to the beach and my conversation with Mark and everything he had tried. Then I backed up and told them about Saturday and getting grounded and my dad meeting Mark.

"Sounds like you did the right thing, sweetie."

"It just scared me so bad. I was sitting there and I suddenly realized if I let him, we could, you know. And I didn't know if I would have done anything about it."

"But you did do something about it," Lori said. "You did great."

"Then why don't I feel great? I feel terrible. I'm never going to have a boyfriend now. Mark's the only guy who's ever been interested in me, and he'll probably never speak to me again."

"That might not be a bad thing," Megan said. "I know it feels awful right now, but you would have felt much more terrible if you had realized the trouble after you had already gone too far."

I blew my nose and leaned back on the couch. "I'm going to have to tell my dad. Aren't I?"

"Do you think you should?" Megan asked.

I nodded sadly.

"Coming clean on the whole thing will make you feel a little bit better," Megan said.

"Now I can't go to prom." I started crying again.

"You could ask Josh," Lori said. "Brian already said he'd take me."

"I don't know. What if Mark brings somebody else?"

"Do you think he will?" Lori asked.

"Maybe. I think he's pretty mad at me. Besides, I may not ever be allowed out of the house again."

I thanked Megan and Lori for talking with me, but I wanted to be home before my dad. I drove home and sat down at the kitchen table and waited. He walked in just after seven thirty.

"Beka. Did you get your errands done?" he asked. He put down his briefcase and stood next to the table. "Are you okay?"

"I need to talk to you," I said. I looked down at my thumbs. I heard him pull out a chair and sit down. I took a deep breath and told him what I had done. I left out some of the details but told him why I got scared and about my conversation with Mark afterwards.

He didn't say anything, but he did keep shifting in his seat.

"Well, you're not going to prom with this boy now," he said when I had finished.

"I already told him I couldn't."

He stood up, making the chair squeak across the tile. "Beka, you do these things, and I don't know whether to be really angry with you or proud of you. You put yourself in a very dangerous situation. He could have taken advantage of you."

"He wouldn't have. He didn't even really try much of anything."

"Well at least you recognized you couldn't handle it. I feel like all I'm doing lately is grounding you."

I spread my fingers out on the table and sighed. "This may not be the time to ask, but could I go to prom with somebody else?"

He looked at me and raised his eyebrows.

"Are you serious? Who?"

"Maybe Josh."

"Only prom, that's it. Other than that you're not doing anything for a long while."

"Really?"

"Well, I'd hate for you to miss your prom."

I stood up and walked around the table and hugged him. He smoothed my hair with his hand and kissed the top of my head. He squeezed me tight, and it was several minutes before he let me go. When he did, his eyes were red and glassy.

"I'm sorry," I said.

"I know. We'll get through this."

He let me go upstairs. Dad hadn't said anything about my phone, so I dialed Josh's number and then hung up. I remembered he had said that he didn't like it when girls asked him out because he liked to do the asking. How was I going to get him to ask me?

I picked up my Bible and opened to Ephesians. I read the whole thing straight through. It was exactly what I needed.

\*　　\*　　\*

Things were weird at school the next morning. Not just because Mark ignored me, but also because it seemed like people were whispering and pointing at me. I even had two guys ask me for my phone number before second period. I grabbed Lori before English and asked her if I was losing my mind.

"I'm afraid not. I heard something this morning."

"What?"

She crinkled her nose. "I don't want to repeat it."

"What do you mean? What did you hear?"

"I heard somebody say something about you finally having, you know, sex."

"What! Please tell me you didn't hear that."

She nodded. "More than once I'm afraid."

"Why? Why would people be saying that? And why is that big news anyway?"

Lori shrugged.

"I want to go home. Please tell me I can go home."

"It's not going to do any good." She grabbed my arm and pulled me toward class. "Come on. You can do it."

As soon as we walked into English, I was greeted by some low whistles and a few catcalls. Gretchen was grinning from ear to ear. My cheeks grew hot, and the anger flashed up inside of me.

I walked straight over to Gretchen and planted my hands on her desk. "Did you do this?" I asked.

"Who me?" Gretchen laughed. "Not even I could have spread this one that fast. So tell me, Beka. How was it?"

I pushed off of her desk and went and sat toward the back. Those hoping for a fight voiced their disappointment and went back to their seats.

Gretchen turned and grinned at me, then gave me a thumbs-up. "Welcome to the club," she giggled.

I could hardly breathe. Gretchen could be lying, but was it possible? Could Mark have told people that we had slept together?

By lunchtime I was ready to put a sign around my neck. I had resorted to simply saying, "It's not true." Even though nobody seemed to believe me. I spotted Mark on the way to the cafeteria and headed for him.

He didn't react when he saw me.

"What is going on?" I asked him.

"What? You think I did this?"

"I don't know what to think. All I know is that the whole school thinks something about me they shouldn't be thinking. And guys have been hitting on me all day."

He laughed and then stopped when he realized I wasn't. "Beka, it's not a big deal. It's only news because you're so . . . so . . ."

"What?"

"Not that type of girl. That's all. It'll blow over."

"Easy for you to say," I said.

"Would it help if I told people it wasn't true?" he asked.

"You mean you're not already?" I said loudly enough to turn a few heads.

"It's not anybody's business."

"But if you don't at least deny it, they'll assume it's true." I threw my hands up in the air. "Do you not care about this at all?"

"It'll all be over with by tomorrow." He took a step toward me. "Can we talk about yesterday?"

I folded my arms. "What about it?"

"Would you reconsider? At least about the prom?"

"It's not an option. My dad knows about yesterday, and he won't let me go with you. And I told you, I need some time."

"How much time?" He was close now and he reached out for my elbow.

"I don't know. I have to get my life with God straightened out. I have to figure out what I'm doing. Having you in my life just makes everything seem so confusing. I really like you, but I just can't right now."

It felt like someone else was using my mouth to talk. Even as I heard the words in my ears, I could hardly believe I was saying them. I wanted to throw my arms around him and ask him to run away with me. But I didn't. He just smiled sadly at me and waved good-bye. I left for the cafeteria, sidestepping a tall greasy-haired guy grinning at me.

I just wanted the day to end.

Lori tried to reassure me at lunch that it would all blow over, but I wanted to defend myself. It would have been easy to do what they all were saying. I felt like I had made a harder choice, and I wasn't getting any credit for it.

Right after lunch I went to see the Young Believers give their presentation in health. I was actually really interested in seeing it. Heidi greeted me at the door and led me to a seat at the side of the room. I took out my notebook to take notes.

After it was over, I thanked Heidi in the hallway.

"So will you join us for the program? We'd like everybody who's willing to take a stand on abstinence to be with us on stage," Heidi said to me.

"Oh, well, I shouldn't if I'm doing the article."

"Oh. I see," she said, but I could tell she didn't see, and I left feeling guilty. It didn't help that Raz Moriano made rude gestures at me when I passed him in the hallway. All of his friends laughed, and I even saw Gretchen and Mai standing in the hallway whispering and giggling. Mai let her silky black hair cover her face as she turned to say something else to Gretchen. I practically ran out of the hallway and straight into Liz.

Liz, even though she was friends with Gretchen, had acted differently ever since the fire at The Snack Shack. She had her smooth blonde hair twisted back into a ponytail that she flipped behind her when she came up to me.

"Hey Beka." She shifted her bag on her shoulder. "So. I heard."

"It's not true. And tell anybody who will listen that it's not true."

"Really? Gretchen said she saw you and Mark at the beach." Liz cocked her head as if she was surprised I denied it.

"I knew it was her. She saw us kiss, but that's it. Nothing else happened."

"Oh. Why does it bother you? I mean, everybody has sex," Liz said.

"No, not everybody does. Actually there are plenty that don't."

She looked behind me and moved to leave. "Well, I'll talk to you later, Beka." She smiled and lifted her hand to say good-bye. I shook my head and kept walking. I still had two more classes to get through.

I tried to avoid Mai and Gretchen and some of the other girls in journalism class, but their snickers were hard to ignore. I couldn't decide if the day had made me completely paranoid or if everybody really was talking about me. I tried to concentrate on the three pages of notes I had taken at the "Wisdom Says Wait" program, but all I did was draw loops around the edge of my notes. Why did all this seem to matter so much all of a sudden? Now I understood why Nancy had said it was smart to think about the physical stuff before you have a relationship with somebody. I would have agreed with Mark's "let's just see what happens" attitude a few weeks ago. Now? Now I knew exactly what would happen.

I was glad I had taken a stand. But I wasn't sure that I really was doing it for some noble spiritual purpose or because I felt God told me to. It was more because I was scared. Not just of what could happen, but of what I saw in myself. I never in a million years would have thought I could be one of those girls who sneaks around and sleeps with her boyfriend any chance she gets. Now I understood. Sex was like skiing. Even if you're just standing at the top of the slope looking down, it's only a short step till you're headed downhill. And stopping was hard. Way harder than I would have expected. I had no doubt that Mark would have kept going. He knew exactly what he was doing. He had been down the slope before.

I wrote the word "Weak" at the top of a blank sheet of paper. My thoughts were spinning around, and I wanted to try and capture what I was feeling.

*Weak*
*I would have followed you*
*into the darkest places*
*Straight down a path I swore I'd never go*
*I would have made a promise*
*One I'd never keep*
*And my heart would never belong to me*

*Where do I go when I'm*
*Too weak to stand*
*Too strong to fall*
*Too sad to cry*
*Too weak to call*
*Can Your mercy find me even here?*

*All my life*
*Is so unclear*
*Can You make my eyes to see?*

*I'd like to know the purpose*
*Of this life of mine*
*I'd like to know there's more to life than this*

*If I see where I need to go*
*But can't find my way*
*Can You carry me until my legs are strong?*

I looked at the paper and smiled. I wished I could make it into music. Music is exactly what I needed to make the thought complete. I laughed as I realized it was Mark who had offered to teach me to play the guitar. That wasn't an option, though. I couldn't be in a small practice room with him every week. But that didn't mean I couldn't learn music.

*     *     *

After dinner, I cornered Dad in the kitchen.

"I wanted to ask you something. About my birthday," I said.

He smiled and wrinkled his eyebrows at the same time. "You're still grounded," he said.

"I know that. But you're still going to get me something, aren't you?"

He leaned back on the sink and folded his arms. "What do you have in mind?"

"I want a guitar. An acoustic one. And lessons."

"Hmmm. That's interesting." He nodded slowly as he thought. "I think we can do that."

"Really? Cool. And I want to go to Haiti with the church in June."

At that one, Dad walked over and sat down at the kitchen table and gestured for me to sit.

"You hadn't said anything else about it, so I just thought you had changed your mind."

I went over to my backpack by the door and retrieved the papers about it and handed them to my dad. "This is what they gave us at the meeting."

"So you want to start guitar lessons and go to Haiti. Why all of a sudden? What's going on?"

"I think I just need a change. Stuff's been happening at school and no I don't want to talk about it, and I'm going to be grounded forever anyway. I just need something new. A change."

"You won't be grounded forever."

"But you haven't said how long, and you're never going to trust me again." I folded my arms on the table and laid my head on them.

"Never say never. It's been rough lately, I know. But we'll get through this. You just keep surprising me, Beka. I never expected any of this from you."

"That makes two of us."

"I have to ask. Have you seen Mark lately?"

"Just at school."

"Well, what did you decide about prom?"

"I'm not going. Josh doesn't like to be asked by girls, so I don't want to have to ask him. It'd be weird."

"I'll look over this trip information and get back to you."

I picked up my head. "And being grounded?"

"We'll see." He put the papers on the counter and went back to the dishes.

I went to my room. School was almost over anyway.

*     *     *

School got only slightly better as the week dragged on. I was still getting rude comments from some guys, and Gretchen was still acting bizarre. The "Wisdom Says Wait" program was really good, and Heidi did a terrific job considering how everybody acted. Ever since the sixth grade, when I remember hearing that JoEllen and Robby had done it, kids talked about sex. I never knew whether they were lying or not. Some of them probably were, but I had always thought most everybody was sexually active. Heidi had said in her talk that almost half of teenagers are virgins until they are at least seventeen years old. So apparently, not everybody was doing it. She also made a good point about how television and movies make it seem like everybody naturally falls into bed with each other.

I saw Nancy and Josh go up on stage afterwards, along with maybe fifty other kids, to take a stand for abstinence. I snapped a few more pictures as it was ending and then went up toward the front so that I could see them both.

Josh gave me a killer smile, but what I noticed most was that Nancy seemed to be nicer. Not that she was ever mean, but ever since the homeschool dance she had been a little distant. She now seemed more like the regular old Nancy.

"Hey you two! I'm glad you came," I said when we had moved to a corner where we wouldn't be trampled.

"Yeah, how come you weren't up there with us?" Nancy said as she pushed my shoulder gently.

I put my hand over my heart. "A reporter must remain a neutral observer."

"Yeah sure, keep telling yourself that," Nancy said.

Josh gave Nancy a look and then she said, "I should go find Heidi and thank her for putting this on. I'll meet you at the car." She pointed at Josh and then disappeared into the crowd.

Josh stepped a little closer and pushed his hands into his jeans pockets. His hair had gotten a bit longer, and it fell across his forehead. I had the urge to brush it to the side but decided to close my notebook and click my pen cap instead.

"I noticed all the signs about the prom when I came in today," he said.

My heart dropped into my stomach, and I bit the inside of my lip.

When I didn't say anything he continued, "I was just wondering if, well, if you would consider letting me take you to your prom."

I knew my eyes sparkled, but I suppressed the smile.

"I mean, you went with me to my dance, so . . ."

"You really wouldn't mind going to a high school prom? With all of these . . . heathens?" I whispered.

He laughed. "That's not how I think of you public school kids. Promise. Seriously though, could I take you?"

I smiled. "I'd like that."

He smiled back, and we stood that way for a minute or so, oblivious to the noise and movement around us. Then he moved just slightly and looked down at his feet. "Nancy'll be waiting," he said.

"Sure. That's fine. I have to get back to class anyway." I lifted up my notebook. "And I have to get this article written."

He said good-bye, and I walked slowly back to my locker to get my books. What a shame. Maybe I should look into Seattle Pacific myself.

\*    \*    \*

I sat at one of the computers during journalism and typed my article, ignoring Gretchen and Mai. I wrote about the group's health presentations as well as the assembly. Even though I knew good journalists were supposed to keep their own opinions out of their work, I couldn't resist adding something to the end.

High school can be a difficult place to learn who you want to be in this life. With so many opinions about what we should and shouldn't do, as well as the expectations of our peers, it can be hard to make wise choices—choices we won't regret even just a few years from now. The Young Believers made many strong arguments for keeping pure, and it's hard to argue with their stance that wisdom really does say to wait.

"Ahhh, now isn't that cute, Mai? She's saying we should wait to have sex. Wasn't Mark any good?"

I whirled around and stood up to face Gretchen. Mai stepped back just slightly and stared at me, almost daring me to speak. Gretchen hardly noticed me as she continued to try to read the article.

"I didn't do anything with Mark, Gretchen. Quit telling people I did."

Gretchen leaned over and whispered in my ear. "I wouldn't argue about it. It's been good for your reputation."

"I don't want a reputation, Gretchen. I want people to know the truth."

"Truth. Hmmm. I seem to recall that there is plenty of truth left to be told."

I swallowed hard. "Gretchen."

She stared at me for a long minute and then smiled wickedly. "Maybe you just need to see what a real guy is like, Beka. We're having a party tonight. Why don't you come and see how the big girls play?"

"I've been to your parties, Gretchen. And I'm not interested."

"Puh-lease. Beka, you passed out long before the real fun began."

Mai continued to stare, shifting her hips every once in a while. Gretchen shrugged, then turned to go. She looked over her shoulder and said, "We'll talk soon." She walked away with Mai right behind her.

I slid back into my chair and turned to face the computer screen. It would be so much easier if people actually said what they meant. I had no idea what Gretchen was up to, but it couldn't be good.

*　　*　　*

When I was at my locker, Liz came up and leaned on the one next to mine.

"What's up?" I asked.

"That assembly was pretty interesting," she said.

"Yeah. I wrote an article about it for the newspaper."

Liz looked at her fingernails for a minute and then looked back at me. "Do you think that what they said, you know, about all those diseases and stuff, do you think that's all true?" she asked.

"Yeah, I mean, Heidi, the girl who did the presentation, she gave me all of her source material. It's all true."

She nodded and began to nibble on her fingernail. I didn't know what else to say. I closed my locker door and smiled at her.

"Well, they said to give this to somebody who could help you, you know. Well, here." She shoved a piece of paper in my hand and then turned and disappeared into the crowd. I unfolded it carefully and read:

"I, Liz Tullin, want to be wise. I will choose to say no to sexual activity of any kind so that I can be free of disease and regret."

She had signed and dated the paper at the bottom. *Why would she give it to me?* I wondered. I folded it back up and put the paper in the outside pocket of my bag.

Before I had even turned down the hallway toward the parking lot, Mark fell into step beside me. I still felt that thrill run through me.

I couldn't help it.

"Please reconsider," he said.

"I can't. My dad is not going to let me go with you." I thought about showing up with Josh, and my stomach flipped over. I knew I had to keep my distance from Mark, but destroying any and all hope was another matter entirely.

He took my shoulder, moved me to the side of the hall and faced me.

"I'm not going to keep chasing you."

"I know. But I told you. I need some time."

He folded his arms and his lips tightened. I took a small step toward him, but he made no move toward me.

"I'm sorry," I mumbled.

"Yeah, so am I." The words came out hard, and then he turned and strode down the hallway. I wanted to chase him, make him understand. Ask him to wait till I figured everything out. But instead, I watched him walk away, as I stood frozen to the spot. I stayed that way until two guys behind me made some foul comments, and one of them tugged on the back pocket of my jeans. I pulled away and walked in the other direction. When was this going to end?

\*　　　\*　　　\*

I saw Paul standing by my car in his baseball uniform. He was looking around anxiously until he spotted me. I sped up just a little to get over to him. His jaw was tight and his face was red as if he'd been running, but it didn't take long to see that was not the reason he looked like that.

"Beka. They . . . What . . ." He stopped and took a deep breath. I watched him clench and unclench his fist. "I heard something today. About you."

I opened the door to my car and threw in my bag. "They've been saying it all week. Where have you been?"

"I didn't hear it until today. I overheard it actually. Andy said . . . I won't tell you what he said. But I almost . . ." He clenched his fist again. His eyes were wide and they darted around as he seemed to process his thoughts. "Is it true?" he choked out.

"What? You can't be serious, Paul!"

"Well!"

"Just because we were together doesn't mean we did anything. Please! I can't believe you thought I would do that." I narrowed my eyes at him and folded my arms.

Paul visibly relaxed, his shoulders dropped, and his face softened. "I'm sorry. I had to ask. But what they were saying . . ."

"I know. It's been awful. I've been trying to figure out where we could move to."

"Why didn't you say something to me?"

"Because there's nothing you can do about it. I'm hoping it all just goes away."

"The guys believe it. They think you're fair game now." His jaw tightened again. "I almost decked that guy in the locker room."

I suppressed a smile. "I would have liked to have seen that."

Paul gave me a half smile. "I want to fix this."

"You can't. I can't. I've been denying it, and it almost makes it get worse. I thought it was getting better, but some guy just grabbed my jeans in the hallway." I pointed inside.

"Beka. You can't let people harass you like that. You have to tell somebody."

"Who? What are they going to do about it? It'll just make it worse."

"Promise me that you'll find me if you need help."

"I promise."

He shifted and kicked his shoe on the pavement. "I have to get to practice. Are you going home?" he asked.

I nodded. "I'll be fine. I promise."

I couldn't decide if I was trying to convince him or myself.

When I got home it was after three. I said hello to Mary, the woman who had been helping out around the house ever since my mom died. She was folding laundry in the family room, and after asking how she was doing, I went up to my room. Lori had gone to DC with her family, so I thought about calling Nancy to see what she was up to for the weekend. Even with being grounded, I thought Dad might be willing to let me hang out with Nancy. Before I even got to the phone though, it rang loudly.

"Hello?"

"Beka."

I knew that voice. I closed my eyes and dropped my head back on my shoulders.

"Gretchen."

"I'll get right to the point. Meet me at Bonfire Beach at nine o'clock tonight."

"Can I ask why?"

"You can ask. But all I'll tell you is that it would be in your best interest to be there."

"Well, I can't. I'm grounded and can't leave the house."

"Like that ever stopped you before."

"I can't. Sorry."

"Beka." Her voice shifted a bit to a more conversational tone. "You mentioned today about how you wanted people at school to know the truth. I thought we might need to talk about that. After all, I think I can help."

"What do you mean?"

"The truth, Beka. You want people to know what really happened. Right?"

"Right." I wasn't sure where she was going.

"Well, I'm just not clear on what I should share. I mean, there is so much. There's the whole Mark thing, your psychotic meltdown . . ."

"What?"

"Your little breakdown, remember? Or maybe that's not something you want me to share. See. That's why we have to talk. I need to know what it is you want." Her voice got an edge to it again. "Be there at nine o'clock. It'll be quite a party. You really won't want to miss it."

I heard the line click, and I dropped the phone back

on the cradle and curled up on my bed. My throat felt tight and my stomach knotted up. I stared at my bookshelf and let my eyes wander over the porcelain butterflies and snow globes from different vacations, the books I loved to read when I was growing up. I closed my eyes but I didn't know how to pray, except to whisper, "Help me." Over and over. I knew it was my fault. I was the one who wanted to kill myself. I was the one who snuck off with Mark and made it look like we were doing something wrong. I didn't deserve any help, but I desperately needed it.

*Please forgive me, God. I know I did wrong. I disobeyed my dad, and I got into trouble. You say You forgive us completely if we ask You. Well, I'm asking. I need Your help. I don't know what to do.*

I don't know how long I lay there, but I didn't get an answer. I don't know what I was expecting, but I still felt unsure when I sat back up. I had to go meet Gretchen. At the very least I had to try and convince her not to tell everybody about my hospital stay. I still had my entire senior year to get through. The teasing about my supposed sexual activity was bad enough. I couldn't bear for the whole school to know about the hospital.

Now how was I going to get out to that party?

I decided to just tell the truth. I needed to convince my dad that I had to go. He wouldn't be home for at least a couple of hours, and I wanted to talk to Lori about it. I sat down to call Nancy instead. She would pray for me and maybe even have a suggestion.

"Hello." I was pretty sure the voice was Josh's but not positive.

"Is Nancy there please?" I asked.

"She's not home right now. Can I take a message for her?"

"No. That's okay."

"Beka? Is that you?"

"Yeah."

"It's Josh. What's up?"

"Oh, nothing. I just . . . I don't know. I needed some advice and I thought Nancy might be able to help."

"Well, is there anything I could do?"

I considered that. Maybe he could help. If Josh and Paul took me to the party, Dad would be much more likely to let me go. I had a terrible feeling about going, but if they went with me, maybe I wouldn't be so scared.

"Maybe. Can you go out tonight?"

"What?"

"Oh, I mean, I'm not trying to ask you out. It's just I need someone to take me to a party. I thought maybe you and Paul could take me."

"Why? What's going on?"

"It's Gretchen. Remember I told you about her."

"Yeah, the girl you were worried about that might do something to you."

"Yeah." I switched the phone to my other ear. "Well, she kind of threatened me tonight. And I have to go to this party to talk to her or else she'll spread more rumors about me."

"Whoa. More rumors? She threatened you? Beka, maybe you should just stay away from her."

"It's not that simple." I didn't want to tell him about what people were saying at school, or about the hospital, but he was moving three thousand miles away. Did it really matter if he knew? And I knew he wouldn't tell anybody else. But I also liked him, and I didn't want him to know those things about me.

"Beka? Are you still there?"

"Yeah. Okay. Well, here's the part of the story I didn't tell you." He listened quietly while I told him the rumors about Mark and me, stressing the fact that they were only rumors, and about my stay at the hospital. I kind of wished I had told him in person so I could see his eyes and his face. I couldn't tell how he was reacting. Would he think I was awful?

"I have to try and talk her out of it. It's been so bad at school, and it would get much worse if this gets out."

"Wow. I had no idea. I'm so sorry."

"So will you go?" I asked.

"Sure. I'll go."

"Thanks. I'll call you in a couple of hours if that's okay so that we can work out the details." I didn't add that I had to run off to my counseling appointment. I figured I had dropped enough on him.

\*       \*       \*

When I settled onto the couch in Julie's office, I proceeded to spill the events of the week to her. I didn't mind talking to her and actually had started to look forward to seeing her. I liked Julie and hadn't stopped trying to find the right time to get her and my dad together.

"So what do you think will happen tonight at this party?" she asked. She slid her pen between her lips and leaned back in her chair. She was wearing a deep purple suit with a multicolored scarf. Her hair was short and pulled partway back.

"I don't know. I just know I should try to talk her out of it. Shouldn't I?"

"Will it do any good?"

I leaned my head back on the couch. "Probably not. She'll tell people when she wants to tell them. But maybe I can delay the inevitable."

"Why are you so worried to have people find out?"

I picked my head back up and looked at her, shaking my head.

"Is it really that awful?" she asked.

"Yes! Boys may get beat up and stuff like that, but girls kill with words."

"But could you get through it? Say Gretchen does tell the whole school you wanted to kill yourself and you stayed at the psych hospital. Could you get through it?"

I considered that. Lori knew and would still be my friend. But all the name calling and being ostracized for who knows how long; it would make it hard to go to or even care about school.

"I guess I'd get through it. It just would make everything so miserable. So completely miserable. If I had a choice, I'd want to keep it a secret."

"It can wear us out to keep secrets. It may not be worth the cost."

I left feeling more unsure of talking to Gretchen, but I also thought it couldn't hurt to try. I couldn't read Gretchen anymore. She certainly wasn't acting mad about the fire incident. Maybe there was a chance she wasn't interested in ruining my life.

*    *    *

I cornered Paul as soon as I got home and told him my plan.

"Will you go? Please? And do you think Dad will go for it?"

Paul shook his head. "I think you should just stay away from her. Really, Beka. Sounds like trouble to me."

"That's not the issue, Paul. I am going to talk with her. I have to try. I just want to know if you'll help. Josh already said he'd go. Please?"

He dropped his head for a minute or so then looked back up. "I'll go. But you'll have to ask Dad."

"No problem." I gave Paul a hug and then ran down the stairs to Dad's workshop. He turned at the noise.

"Is the house on fire?" he asked.

"No. But I have to ask you something." I told Dad most of the story, barely stopping to breathe in between. "Josh and Paul are both willing to go with me. I won't get in trouble. I just need to try to sort this out."

Dad turned away and leaned both his hands on his workbench. I thought about throwing out a few more reasons why I had to go, but I just watched him instead. It seemed to take forever.

He walked toward me a few steps and then sat on the metal stool between us.

"Beka."

I could tell by the sound of my name that he didn't want me to go.

"Dad please? Do you remember at all what high school is like? I have to try to fix this. If I don't go, Gretchen will spread even more rumors."

"More?"

I had left out the rumors about me. I didn't think Dad could handle hearing that about his oldest daughter.

"She's done it before. She'll make it as sensational as possible, and by the time she gets through with me, I'll look crazier than that guy who dances and sings downtown."

"Paul is willing to go with you?"

I straightened my back. "Yes."

"Alright. You can go. But I expect you to be on your best behavior. And you're still grounded. You can go, talk to Gretchen, and then come home. Got it?"

"Absolutely. Thanks, Dad!" I ran down the last two stairs, hugged him, and sprinted back up the stairs. I told Paul that Dad had agreed and asked him to call Josh while I changed. I was nervous about talking to Gretchen, but I was even more nervous about seeing Josh. I wished I hadn't spilled my every secret. What would he think of me now?

*　　*　　*

I was ready in record time, which for me was about thirty minutes. I had picked some jeans and a button-down top. Simple but stylish. I definitely didn't want to show any more skin than necessary. It would just add fuel to the fire. Paul was waiting for me in the kitchen. He gave me a look and nodded seriously.

We drove to Josh's house, and he was sitting on the front porch. When he saw us, he jumped up and climbed in the backseat. We didn't say much on the way there, but when we parked at Bonfire Beach, Paul turned off the car, undid his seatbelt, and turned so that he could see both of us.

"We need to pray," Paul said.

We all bowed our heads, and I listened as Paul prayed. It sounded as if he was really talking to God, asking for wisdom and protection and strength. I heard Josh murmur his agreement. I didn't pray out loud, but inside I just asked God to help Gretchen listen to reason, and almost immediately I felt like I shouldn't even bother to try and talk to her. I somehow knew it wasn't going to do any good at all. But after Paul and Josh said "Amen," I just looked at them and smiled.

"Thanks for coming, you guys," I said.

"Are you sure about this?" Paul asked.

I hesitated. Was that God telling me not to go? Or was I just feeling hopeless?

I nodded. "Let's go."

\*       \*       \*

The parking lot was packed with cars. I had only ever been to one party at Bonfire Beach before. Celia, who had been my best friend before she moved away, and I had come to one the year before my mom had died. It was a very complicated event because they couldn't have any alcohol in sight since the police were always coming by. The bonfire was legal however, and, technically, the beach was private property, so they left things alone as long as there weren't any visible problems. Celia and I didn't stay long that night, but it looked pretty similar as the three of us made our way to the beach. I spotted Gretchen almost immediately. She raised her eyebrows when she saw me and moved over and whispered something to Mai. Mai glanced my way and then turned and walked away.

"Beka. I'm going right over there." Paul pointed to where some of his teammates were lounging on the beach just a few yards from the fire. Between the fire and the full moon, I could even see their faces. "If you need anything, I'll be right there."

I nodded. "I'll be fine. I'll find you if I need you."

Paul moved over to his friends and Josh stepped close.

"Do you want me to stay with you?" he asked.

I smiled. "Nah. You can hang with Paul. I'll find you guys after I talk to Gretchen."

He let his head drop a bit to the side and looked at me softly. Oh how I wished he wasn't going away. His eyes seemed kind and soft, and I was glad to see he hadn't pulled away from me now that he knew my secrets.

"I'll be fine. Really."

He squeezed my elbow, then turned and went over to where Paul was sitting. I took a deep breath and looked around. There were a lot of kids there, and I recognized most of them. As soon as Josh left my side, though, several guys came close enough to knock me off balance and snickered at me. Colin, one of the rich kids, grabbed at the bottom of my shirt and said something rude. I moved away. I just wanted to get it over with.

There were lots of different groups of kids standing around, and many moved back and forth between the beach and the cars. I also saw several groups disappearing into the line of trees at the edge of the beach past the parking lot. The trees were small, but there were lots of them. I was sure they had coolers of something hiding in those trees. The full moon reflected on the water, and I saw some kids playing near the water. Gretchen was dancing with a group on the other side of the bonfire from where I was.

"I'm here," I said when I reached her.

"I can see that." She winked at Jeremy, who was standing nearby.

"Look, Gretchen. I'm not staying, so if you want to talk let's talk."

She cocked her head at me and pulled at a blonde curl. "Relax, Beka. Why don't you go find yourself a drink?"

"I'm leaving." I turned but felt Gretchen grab my arm. I turned back around.

"Well, then, if you're so anxious to get on with it." She laughed, but it wasn't a nice pleasant laugh. It was a laugh that made the hair on the back of my neck stand up. "You know the rock jetty at the end of the beach?"

I nodded.

"Meet me there in fifteen minutes." Gretchen turned and walked over to where Jeremy was standing with Lance and some of the other guys. She lifted her arms above her head and moved her hips as she moved closer to him. I didn't see Mai anywhere. It was just as well. I sat down by the fire as the party raged around me.

Liz came over and sat down next to me. "I didn't expect to see you here."

I smiled and leaned forward on my knees. "Me neither. I have to talk to Gretchen."

She looked over to where Gretchen was still dancing provocatively with Jeremy. Liz shook her head.

"So. About that paper," I said.

"Yeah, well. I thought you might be willing to, you know, ask me if I'm keeping my promise."

"Sure. I guess it just surprised me, that's all."

"Well, I started going to church again, and I guess I just thought that's what I should do. You know?"

I didn't know how to ask her what she meant by going to church. *Was she a Christian?* I wondered. "So how come you decided to go to church?" I asked.

"Well, Gretchen is still into the whole Wicca thing you know, and sometime after the fire we were over at her house, Mai, Theresa, and me, and we were having some sort of séance. Well, Gretchen started talking real weird, and when she cast this spell, the flames from the candles went out suddenly. I don't know. The whole thing freaked me out. So I started going to church with my mom."

I nodded. I checked my watch and realized I should start walking toward the jetty. I didn't really know what else to say to her anyway, so it was a good excuse to get out of there. "So, you gonna be good tonight?" I asked.

Liz laughed. "Danny broke up with me when I said I wanted to cool things off, you know?"

I laughed too and told her I'd see her at school. I liked Liz, but I had to be careful. She was still pretty mixed up with Gretchen's clan, and I didn't know whether to totally trust her.

In just a minute of walking, I had moved past the heat and light of the bonfire into the quiet stillness of the beach. I knew the walk would only take me a few minutes, so I walked slowly and enjoyed the moonlight dancing on the water.

*Lord, I don't know what Gretchen will say, but be with me please. And help me to know You better. I feel like I don't know You yet. I don't know when You're talking to me or if I'm talking to myself. How do I know the difference?*

I reached the jetty, and I sat and turned my back to the water and scanned the beach. There was no one in sight. I couldn't even hear the party even though I knew they were just down the beach. The sand was dimly lit by the moon, but the tree line was just blackness. I shivered. I suddenly wished I had told Paul and Josh where I was. I was at the end of the inlet, so the beach wrapped around the other side. The beach curved too far to the left for me to see where the party was. If I could just see some people, I wouldn't feel so nervous. I tried to let my eyes adjust to see the tree line better, but it was too dark. I shivered again and looked at my watch. Did I have time to run back and tell them where I was?

I jumped up and started walking back toward the party, but as soon as I stood up, I saw three figures moving next to the tree line right toward me. They were coming from the opposite side of the inlet. I could only see their outlines, but none of them looked like Gretchen.

I moved all the way out toward the water where there was more light and eyed the figures moving closer. Maybe they were just heading to the jetty. I picked up my pace, splashing the water just a little bit. As the beach turned I got just a glimpse of the bonfire in the distance and I turned to see where they were behind me. First one began to run, and then the other two started running toward me. I took off at a dead run, the water splashing my back. My shoes slipped off, but it helped me to run faster. I was no match for them.

I turned to see where they were just as someone tackled me into the water. I only got a glimpse of his face, but it looked familiar. I screamed, and I felt a hand clamp over my mouth. It wasn't until that moment that I realized how much trouble I was in. I could see the party down the beach as if it was in miniature. Someone pressed my head into the sand and water, and I felt my hands pinned together behind my back. Someone held a knife in front of my eyes and twirled it slowly.

"See this? Scream one more time and that'll be the last time you scream." He pushed it against the skin underneath my chin. "Are we clear?" I nodded just slightly. I could feel the point of the blade with every movement.

"Do it. Tie it around her head," I heard. The knife disappeared, and I struggled to get my hands free as I thrashed my head and the hand came off my mouth. Before I could even consider screaming though, water filled my mouth and nose. I felt some cloth go around my eyes and then tighten around my head. I got lifted out of the water, and I coughed to clear my throat and nose. I struggled to catch my breath and then let out a scream. A hand was slapped over my mouth and someone whispered fiercely, "I ain't kidding about this." I felt the sharp blade at my stomach as he cursed at me. They forced me to walk forward with my hands pinned behind my back.

My heart was racing. I had to get out of there. I could tell only one of them had hold of me, but the others were close. They were snickering and laughing. Not to mention the knife that was being held under my shirt. Every time I stumbled I could feel it, and I was sure it had cut through my skin already. We had turned away from the direction of the party, and in a moment I felt tree branches scratch at my face as they pushed me deep into the tree line. I was going to die and never be found. Then I realized that there were things even worse than being killed.

*       *       *

"Please, please let me go," I said through the hand over my mouth. They just laughed. And a few moments later they stopped and pushed me down to my knees. As soon as the hand came away from my mouth I screamed. As loudly as I could. A hand went back over my mouth, and someone cursed at me.

"Just hold her mouth."

"Put that stupid knife away."

"There, hold her down there."

The back of my head hit the ground, and I felt hands on me, pulling at my shirt. I felt like I was going to throw up. *Paul? Josh? How are they going to find me?* The cloth over my eyes shut out their faces. *Help me Lord, please help me.* Over and over I pleaded for help.

"What are you doing?"

"We're just supposed to scare her."

All I could smell was the dirty hand pressed across my face as I moved around trying to dislodge it. I sobbed, trying to force my mind to think about anything else. I imagined I was still back talking with Liz and feeling the heat of the fire on my face. I felt like I was swirling down a drain, deeper and deeper into nothingness. Slowly the blackness moved in and brought with it utter and total silence.

*       *       *

A sudden movement jarred me. Was I still here? I could still feel the cloth over my face. How long had I been here? My stomach rolled over as I realized it was all real. Not some nightmare I could wake up from. It only took a moment for every nerve in my body to wake back up and to realize one leg was free. I lifted it and shoved it forward as hard as I could. I connected with somebody as I heard a big "Humphh."

A second later a string of curses flew, and I felt the blade cut across my right side. But before the pain could even register, I heard the sound of my name. *Lord, hear me, please. Rescue me. Is that You, God?*

"Someone's looking for her."

"We ain't done!"

"Let's go. Just leave her."

"Make sure you get everything."

I heard cursing and movement and then nothing.

Except the sound of my name in the distance. I rolled over on my side, not even bothering to pull the cloth off my eyes. I pulled my shirt around me and tried to curl in a ball, but pain seared through my right side. The skin there was warm and sticky. I cried. Out of relief. Out of pain. Out of everything.

I wasn't even sure I wanted to be found.

I listened to my name being called over and over. First Paul, then Josh, then both of them. I reached up and pulled the cloth off my head and rolled onto my back. I couldn't sit up. I could see little patches of sky through the short trees. I pushed the hair out of my face and rested my hand on my forehead. I sobbed quietly.

I wanted to disappear. I didn't want Paul or Josh to see me like this. But I couldn't just stay here either. Why? Why did this have to happen? It seemed so stupid that I came to try to keep Gretchen from talking. I shouldn't have come. It was my own stupid fault.

I rolled over onto my hands and knees, being careful

not to bend at my waist. I stood up slowly, and for just a moment I thought I might pass out. I put myself back together as best as I could. My shirt was torn and bloody, and I could barely make my knees hold me up. I leaned against a tree as my name got louder and louder.

I could see a flashlight through the trees, and then a moment later it shined on my face.

"Beka!"

I collapsed into Paul's arms, and we both slid back down to the ground.

"You're bleeding. Josh, tell me you have a cell phone."

I couldn't even look at Josh, but I heard the musical tones of the phone being dialed.

"Get me out of here, Paul."

"We have to stay, Beka. So the police can come. Who did this to you?"

"I don't care." I cried. "You have to get me out of here."

"Look, I'm staying with you. But we're staying until the police get here."

"But everybody at the party. They'll see."

"No they won't. We'll tell them to keep everybody back, I promise."

He wrapped his arms around me. Josh hovered near us. He had given directions to the 911 person, and after a few minutes he said, "I'm going to stand on the beach so that I can show them where you are."

I peeked over Paul's shoulders to look at Josh's face. I couldn't tell what he was thinking. Was he angry? Or scared?

As soon as Josh moved back through the trees, Paul leaned me away from him. "Let me see you."

I leaned back so he could see my side. "There's too much blood, and I don't have anything clean to wipe it." He moved my shirt back over it and pressed. "It's still bleeding, so we need to keep pressure on it." I groaned as he pushed on it.

"Can you tell me what happened?"

I shook my head.

"Did . . . were you . . . raped?" he choked on the words.

I shook my head hard. "No. I swear. They just . . . You stopped them when you called for me."

"Them. There was more than one?"

I nodded and started crying again.

He pulled me close. "We found your shoes on the beach. I thought you had drowned."

"How did you know where to look?"

"A girl told us you had walked in this direction."

"Liz," I said. "I'm really tired."

"No, Beka. Keep talking to me. They'll be here any minute."

Josh came back and said, "They're right here."

Suddenly I was surrounded. A paramedic slapped open his case, and another one moved Paul away from me and laid me back down in the dirt. Flashlights were everywhere. The police were trying to keep everyone back from the "scene," and the paramedic wiped my side down with something cool and wet.

"It's not too bad, sweetie," he said. "It's pretty deep,

but they'll fix you up at the hospital. Yep. They'll fix you right up."

A policeman shined another light in my face. "Can you tell me what happened, miss?"

"Do I have to?" I asked.

"Can she talk to you later?" Paul stepped forward and offered his hand. "I'm her brother."

"You found her?" he asked. They moved away and turned their backs. I looked up at the patch of sky above me. After the paramedic had packed gauze on my cut, two other men moved me onto a portable stretcher, laid a blanket over me, and began to strap me in. Josh appeared at my side.

I looked away.

He brushed the hair out of my face but didn't say anything.

"Step back, sir," one of the guys said as they lifted me up.

"Don't take me by the party," I said. "Please."

"Don't worry. Everybody took off when we showed up," the man said to me. "No one will see you." He winked at me and patted my arm.

I watched the stars go by above my head, wishing I could disappear into the blackness.

*     *     *

The ride to the hospital was surreal. The paramedic who had first cleaned me up kept trying to make me laugh, but I couldn't. The beach had been deserted when we got to the parking lot. So it wasn't until we pulled into the hospital that I saw someone I knew.

Dad was waiting in the corridor when they pulled me out of the ambulance. As soon as I saw him, I burst into tears, making my side hurt all over again. He ran next to the stretcher as they wheeled me into a small room. They moved me over onto another table, and people swarmed me almost immediately.

"Sir, you'll have to wait outside."

"She's my daughter. I'm staying." I couldn't see him, but I could hear his voice crack.

"Let us do our job. We'll get you in a few minutes."

I felt them pull the gauze off my side and wipe it down again. I heard someone call for a surgical consult.

"Surgery? It's just a little cut, right?"

"We're going to let somebody else take a look at it to make sure."

It didn't hurt as bad, and I felt very tired all of a sudden. A few minutes later another person came in and pulled the padding back again. He prodded and pressed, and then stood up. "Everything looks good. You can close it."

"No surgery?" I asked.

A woman by my head smiled at me. "No surgery. They just had to make sure."

*     *     *

They moved me into another room. My dad followed us there and stood next to me stroking my hair while a man and a woman came to stitch up my side. They called it a three-layer close and kept telling me how lucky I was that the knife didn't go any deeper.

"Well, you've got a grand total of fifty stitches." She sounded impressed.

They left and another nurse came in and told me that a doctor wanted to check me inside.

"Why?"

"To make sure you weren't hurt inside."

"But they didn't. . . . I wasn't raped. Please. I just want to go home."

"Are you sure no one raped you?" She eyed me suspiciously.

"Yes, they just . . . forget it. I'm fine. I don't need to be checked."

She frowned and left the room. I could see her talking to a doctor behind a large counter.

*       *       *

"Beka. Are you sure you're okay? I can go wait out there if you want to . . ."

"Dad, no. It's not that. They didn't rape me."

Dad drew in a long slow breath and blinked his eyes fast. I could see him swallow and tighten his jaw.

"I'm never going to let you out of my sight again. I swear."

"Da-ad."

"If I lock you in your room, nothing can ever happen to you. We'll send your meals up there, and you can use the phone if you want." He smiled for a moment, and then one sob escaped from his throat. "I was so scared," he whispered hoarsely.

I felt my own tears trickling down the side of my face. Dad leaned over and hugged me as best as he could in that position.

*       *       *

After a while a couple of policemen came in and asked me to tell them what happened. I looked at my dad, and he nodded and slipped outside the room. I told them what I could remember. It all had happened so fast. They wanted so many details though, and I spent most of the time staring at the ceiling so I wouldn't have to look at them when I told them.

"Can you describe what any of them looked like?"

I shook my head. "I only saw one of them. And it was so quick. He was the one with the knife."

"What did he look like?" they pressed.

"I don't know. I just remember that he seemed familiar. Like I might know who he is."

"So do you? Do you know him?"

"I can't remember. I'm sorry."

One of them flipped a page back in his notebook. "And this girl you were going to meet? Gretchen? Did she have anything to do with this?"

"No. I don't know." Gretchen? Gretchen was a lot of things, but could she have done this? I fingered the tape around my side.

The policemen gave me their cards and asked me to call if I remembered anything else.

"What's going to happen?" I asked as they walked out.

"Depends on if we catch them," he said. "Take care, miss."

*　　*　　*

A few minutes later Dad came back around the corner with Julie, who looked like she had just come from the gym, standing next to him. I smiled seeing them together. Now that was a much better fit than Gabby any day.

"Sorry honey, I called Julie as soon as I heard from Paul," Dad said.

"That's fine," I told him. I looked at Julie. "Sorry it's so late."

"Greg, can you give us a few minutes?" she asked. My dad nodded and left again, and Julie pulled a rolling stool over and sat where I could turn and look at her. I couldn't sit up very well. She gave me a sympathetic smile, and I immediately burst into tears and told her what happened. She didn't press me for details; she just listened and squeezed my hand.

"So they didn't rape you?" she asked.

"No. Why doesn't anyone believe me? That nurse looked at me like I was deluded earlier."

"A lot of girls that come in here deny anything happened. Even when it did."

"Well, I'm not. Paul and Josh were yelling my name and it scared them off. I guess they might have done more if they had time but . . ."

"How are you feeling now?"

"A little spacey."

Julie smiled. "Well, that's probably the painkillers."

"Numb I guess. Like it didn't happen at all. Like maybe I just had a bad dream."

"That's understandable. They're going to want to keep you here overnight. Is it alright if I come back to see you tomorrow?"

"Sure. But it's Saturday." I took the plunge. "Don't you have a boyfriend to hang out with?"

"No, I don't, if you must know. I'd rather come hang out with you anyway."

I grinned. "Well if you have nothing else to do."

"Alright. I'll see you then. You've got some good-looking guys in the waiting room worried about you."

"One of them's my brother," I said, blushing.

She smiled knowingly and waved good-bye. I expected someone else to come around the door, but I just couldn't keep my eyes open another second.

*O*pen mine next!" Anna said, tripping over Lucy to get to my spot on the couch.

I took her gift and she jumped up next to me. I tried to unwrap it carefully, but it looked like she had used an entire roll of tape on the small package.

I lifted off the cover and picked up a bright silver whistle hanging from a red rope necklace. Anna grabbed it from me and slipped it over my head.

"It's for in case someone tries to hurt you again. You just blow this." She blew the whistle, making everyone in the room cover their ears. "And everyone'll know you need help."

I kissed the top of her head and smoothed her red hair. "That's a great gift, Anna. Thanks."

Lori laughed and brought me another box. "Now that will go perfect with my gift." She put the box on my lap and sat back down on the floor. I opened it to find a mini blow horn and a can of pepper spray.

I laughed. "I told you all I'll be more careful! Seriously, thanks. This is the perfect birthday."

And I meant it. Things seemed good. Dad was actually smiling and laughing. It was almost a relief, because he had seemed so worried. Then again, it may have been more than just me getting better. Every time Dad brought me to Julie's office, and I went at least four times since the attack, I thought there was some definite eye dancing going on between them. And then there was Josh, who was sitting on the floor next to Paul. I had lost count of all the flowers Josh had sent me over the last couple of weeks. And he and Paul looked like they had become close. Life had possibilities.

"Well, I have a gift for you too, you know." Dad reached behind the couch and pulled out a guitar case with a bright red bow wrapped around it.

I squealed. "You got one for me!"

Dad laid the case on the floor and snapped it open. He took out a beautiful wood acoustic guitar and handed it to me. I strummed the strings and cringed.

"Don't worry. I've already arranged for lessons." He smiled. "Do you like it?"

"It's perfect," I said. I tried to find the chord Mark had showed me. It took a couple of tries, but finally it sounded right.

"And this kind of goes with that," Lucy said as she handed me a gift bag.

I set the guitar down next to me and pushed aside the tissue paper in the bag. I pulled out a long leather guitar strap with a butterfly embroidered on it.

"This is beautiful, Lucy. Thank you!" She leaned down to give me a hug.

We spent the rest of the evening playing games and then watched a movie, my pick. Lori and I whispered through the whole movie. I was a little disappointed because Josh hadn't brought me anything for my birthday, and I complained to Lori about it. It's not that I wanted more presents. I just wanted to see what he would bring.

But after Lucy and Anna had gone to bed, and Megan had come to pick up Lori, Josh came up to me in the kitchen. "Can you go for a short walk?"

I looked over at my dad, who was loading the dishwasher with the glasses and plates from the party, and asked him if I could go.

"Don't get too tired," he said.

"It's much better, Dad. I'm fine."

Josh and I walked down to the corner and back, talking about the beautiful weather, the prom, which was only a week away, and the gifts I had been given. When we got back to the house, he sat me down on the porch swing and then said he would be right back.

I liked having him around, but it still felt a little weird being with him. I felt like when he looked at me, he saw me that night, imagining what those guys had done to me. He never brought it up, and I certainly didn't want to. Yet he had stayed close, calling, being around. I felt like that night messed me up somehow. That I wasn't worth the same anymore. Not to mention that Josh would be surrounded by beautiful, intelligent college girls who would certainly give him plenty of attention. I had to just let him go. I wanted to enjoy the prom. But then I had to just let him go.

He smiled as he came back up on the porch with a box wrapped with shimmery purple paper and a big purple bow on top. Not too heavy, but not light either.

I unwrapped it slowly and lifted off the lid. Inside I found boxes and packages of stationery. The first box had yellow paper with funky butterflies in the corners. Another package was pale vellum paper with my name written in script at the top. I fingered the embossing and then lifted up another box. This one had pictures from Thomas Kincaid printed on the outside of folded note cards. The last package had paper with tiny butterflies all around the outside border. At the bottom were several packages of pens. I looked up at him.

"This is my way of asking you if you would write to me. When I go away."

"E-mail is quicker," I said.

"But it's not the same. Would you?"

I shrugged. "Yeah, I guess. Are you sure though? I guess I think of college being some big new adventure. I don't want you to feel obligated."

"I want to do this." He put his hand over the top of mine. It made me catch my breath, but I didn't pull away. "I've been praying about this for a long time." He gestured toward the box with his chin. "This is what I felt God tell me."

"He told you we should write each other?" I looked at the stationery with my name on it.

"Sort of. It's up to you if you want to write back. But I want to write to you."

I nodded and slid the top back on the box. "Thanks."

It looked like he was about to say something and then changed his mind. We said our good-byes, and I watched his car pull out of the driveway. I stood there for a while. I had to keep my distance.

When I went back inside, I found that Dad was still in the kitchen, and he was making some tea. I climbed up on one of the stools, leaned my elbows on the counter, and put my chin in my hands. "Thanks for the guitar. I love it."

"I'm glad. You'll have to call the music store to arrange for your lessons. I wasn't sure which day would be best for you."

"I will."

He stirred his tea and looked at me.

"You okay?" he asked.

"I don't know. I have to go back to school tomorrow." I ran my finger along the edge of the counter.

"I don't think you should miss any more school."

"Oh, I know. It's just, what if the guys who did it go to my school? What if . . ."

Dad moved over next to me and wrapped his arms around me. There was nothing either of us could do. I felt so helpless. I had felt safe at the hospital and at home.

I didn't know if I was ready to go anywhere. Especially school.

Dad stroked my hair and began to pray, "Lord, please help Beka to feel Your presence with her. Help her to know Your peace and comfort. And we ask that You protect her from harm. Keep her safe as she finishes out this school year. Keep her safe."

He squeezed tighter. *Keep her safe.* If God didn't protect me that night, why would He protect me at school? Something even worse could happen. The police didn't have any real good leads. They kept asking me if I remembered anything about the one guy, but I couldn't. When I tried to think about it, his face fell into a shadow. Dad pulled back and looked in my eyes.

"I don't know what to do to help you," he said.

I shrugged. I didn't know either. All of the happy feelings that had surrounded me for the birthday party had been replaced by a black cloud that followed me as I went to my room and crawled into bed. I curled into a ball and tried to think about nothing.

\*　　\*　　\*

"Stop!" I screamed and sat up in bed, out of breath and dripping with sweat. When I realized I was in my room, my breathing started to slow. Dad tossed open my door and ran over to my bed. Paul, Lucy, and Anna all appeared in the doorway.

"What happened? What's wrong? Are you okay?" Dad asked. His eyes were wide, and his hair was sticking up.

"I . . . I think so." I pulled the covers up across my shoulders. My heart was still pounding.

Anna came over to the other side of the bed. "You screamed really loud."

I looked at her and then back at my dad.

"Okay, she's fine. You all go back to bed." Paul, Lucy, and Anna left, and Dad sat down on my bed. "Can I get you anything?"

I shook my head. I couldn't stop shaking. I clenched my teeth to keep them from chattering. I looked at the clock. It was only one in the morning.

Dad prayed for me and then left me to go back to sleep.

*       *       *

At three everybody was back in my room, and we did the whole thing over again.

"I'm sorry," I said.

"It's okay." Dad rubbed his hand through his hair and sent everybody back to bed again. He prayed for me again and left.

*       *       *

At four and then again at five, Dad shuffled back in my room. Lucy and Anna stopped coming, but Paul leaned in the doorway looking tired. Dad would check to make sure I was okay and then tuck the covers around me. I didn't bother trying to go to sleep after that. I watched the numbers on my digital clock tick by one number at a time until it was time to get ready for school.

I got dressed slowly and went downstairs. Dad and Paul looked tired, and Lucy and Anna kept asking me what my nightmares were about. I lied to them and told them I couldn't remember.

I was tired but doing okay until we started walking to the door, and then I felt like I couldn't catch my breath. The door seemed farther and farther away, and my heart was being squeezed inside my chest. My heart was racing and it hurt, making me double over. I felt hot all over, as if I had been running forever. I thought for sure I was having a heart attack. Dad and Paul sat me on the floor. I couldn't take a deep breath, and when I tried it was like a knife going through me.

Dad was about to call an ambulance when it started to subside.

"No, don't. I think I'm okay." I held my hand across my chest and tried to breathe. Paul stared at me wide-eyed, and Dad was still holding the phone. "I think I'm okay now."

After a few more minutes, Dad sent Paul along to school, and he called Julie while I sat on the floor breathing slowly. I felt much better, but I didn't understand what had happened. It couldn't be a heart attack at seventeen.

"Julie said it was probably a panic attack. She wants us to come in at lunchtime."

"A panic attack?" I asked.

"I'll call Mary to come early so somebody's here with you. I'll come to take you to Julie's at lunchtime."

"It's gone now. You don't have to worry."

He didn't listen. Mary was there within a half an hour, and I was tucked back into bed. I couldn't settle my thoughts, so I snuck downstairs after a while and got on the computer to look up panic attacks. There was all this stuff about panic disorder, posttraumatic stress disorder, and anxiety. My heart was thumping again just thinking about it. I signed off and went upstairs feeling scared. Was something wrong with me? I mean, really wrong with me?

\*　　\*　　\*

Julie had a pinched look on her face as I described what happened that morning.

"Has anything else happened? Your dad said you woke up screaming last night."

"Yeah. Nightmares."

"What were they about?" she asked.

"I can't remember." I pushed the images out of my head. I didn't want to think about the attack anymore. I just wanted it all to go away. "I don't understand. What happened to me?"

Julie leaned forward. "Are you worried about going back to school?"

I shrugged. "I'm not looking forward to it, but it's not some huge deal. Why?"

"I'm not sure. But you're probably just having a reaction to your attack. Chances are it won't happen again anyway."

"Really?"

"Yeah. And I think it would be good for you to go back to school now. I know there's only a couple of hours left, but you should get it over with."

*       *       *

I didn't have any problems as I checked into the office. When I arrived at my locker, I found notes and flowers taped all over the outside of it. I read each one. Some were signed and some weren't. They said things like, "Welcome Back!" "You Rock!" and various quotes about courage and strength. I smiled. It was such an unexpected surprise. It meant everybody knew. The paper never released my name, but it wasn't hard to figure out. I gathered my books and headed to journalism.

I pushed open the door, and everyone in the room stopped talking and turned to look at me. I stood there awkwardly, not sure whether to keep moving or wait until they moved. Then Jen, our student editor, started clapping, and then one by one the rest of the room joined her, including Ms. Adams. I looked around at each of them somewhere between tears and laughter. I noticed Mai and Gretchen standing in the corner with their arms folded. They didn't look happy.

Ms. Adams lifted up her hands. "Okay everybody. Let's get busy. We have a deadline." Everybody went back to work, and Ms. Adams came over to me and led me to my usual seat. She talked with me for a minute to see what I wanted to do. Once I assured her I could do some work and that I was fine, she gave me some articles to proofread.

"If you need anything. Anything at all. You let me know, okay?" she said.

I smiled and nodded at her, but as soon as she left my side, Gretchen came over and pulled a chair up next to my desk.

Gretchen had a funny, anxious look in her eye when she sat down. "Aren't you the queen today? It'll pass."

"What do you want, Gretchen?" I tapped my pencil on the papers in front of me.

"Just wondering what really happened. There must be a million stories being floated."

"And why would I tell you?"

Gretchen protested with a huffy sigh. "Oh please, Beka. I could get everything cleared up. Who better to spread the real story?"

I eyed her. "I don't want to talk about it."

"Come on. Tell me. I'll tell people the truth. I promise."

"You promise? You promise?" I could hear my voice going up. "Where were you that night? I was there and you weren't. What, did you forget? Or were you ever planning on coming?"

Her eyes narrowed. "I know you're not accusing me of having anything to do with this."

"Maybe I am. For all I know you sent those guys there to find me and . . ." My voice shook and I could feel my face getting hot. Several kids were watching us now.

"What? You can't think that." She put her hand over her heart and widened her eyes.

"Missing the spotlight, Gretchen?" I asked. Another small group had gathered near us. I kept going. "You just had to get your revenge, didn't you? Well you went too far, Gretchen."

Her face tightened. "Don't make an enemy of me, Rebekah Madison. You'll lose. I promise you that."

She flipped her hair and looked away, and in that instant my mind flashed to that day in the parking lot when she tried to run me over. I could see her sitting in her Jeep. . . . My stomach swirled, and I jumped from my desk and ran from the room covering my mouth. That face that kept falling into shadow suddenly had a name.

# In the bathroom

I scrubbed my face in the sink and used my hand to scoop some water into my mouth. I felt so sick. I just wanted to run. Run and never stop. Leave this place, these people. I had to get out of there. I didn't know what to do. My heart was racing again. I frantically thought about where Paul would be. I had to get home. I looked around the bathroom and realized I only had ten minutes before the halls filled with kids.

I threw open the door and ran down to the science wing. Paul had physics, didn't he? I passed the windows slowly, looking for my brother's face. I spotted him through the third window, but he was intently writing. A second later, though, a guy next to him looked at me and then turned and tapped my brother on the shoulder. Paul looked up and then jumped out of his chair. He came into the hallway a moment later.

"What is it? What's wrong?" He held my shoulders.

"Please take me home," I whispered.

"Stay right here." He disappeared back in the class-room and then came back out with his backpack. "Let's go." He took a firm hold of my elbow and steered me down the hallway. We were just two steps from the door when the bell echoed through the halls. I began to run, and Paul sped up to jog alongside of me. We dove into the car, and Paul tore out of the parking lot. As soon as we hit the main road, he glanced over at me.

"You okay?" he asked.

I nodded and leaned my head back against the seat. I tried to take slow calm breaths to slow my heart and my breathing.

"What happened?" he asked.

I shook my head, not opening my eyes. He didn't say anything else, and when we got home he took me to my room. I crawled into bed and pulled the covers over my head. I couldn't stop my hands from shaking. I folded them up underneath my arms. I pushed every thought from my head. I just wanted to sleep. I wanted to sleep and think about nothing.

\*        \*        \*

When I woke up it was dark outside. I hadn't had any nightmares, and when I turned over on my back, I was relieved to find my heart beating normally and that panicky feeling gone. For the moment anyway. There was a sweaty glass of water sitting on my nightstand. I grabbed it, drank every drop, and then scooted back against the headboard and held my pillow in my lap. I didn't want to think. I sat there for a while until my mind wandered back to the nights Celia and I had sat on this bedspread, talking and painting our nails. I remembered my mom hanging the butterfly border around my room, wearing her splattered overalls and her hair in a ponytail. I clutched my arms around my stomach and dropped my head. Maybe it was good that my mom couldn't see me like this.

A little while later, the doorknob turned very slowly and the door creaked open. Dad's face poked around the door, and when he saw me, he rushed over and sat on my bed.

"You're up. How are you?"

I shrugged my shoulders. I couldn't make my throat work. The images of the attack kept trying to force their way into my thoughts.

"Can you tell me what happened?"

I shook my head. I had left my backpack in journalism. I didn't have any books. Did I have homework to do?

Dad rubbed his hands on his pants. "Can I get you some dinner?"

I shook my head again and leaned back. I closed my eyes. I felt tired all over again.

"Please talk to me, Beka. You're scaring me. Just tell me something. Anything."

What could I say?

"Do you want me to call Julie?" he asked.

I shook my head.

"Let me put it this way. Would you mind if I called Julie?"

I shrugged. It didn't matter. I didn't want to talk to anybody. I just wanted it all to go away. Go back to sleep and let the darkness sweep me away.

He got up to leave. "I'll check on you soon, okay?"

I opened my eyes. "Are you going to go out with her?"

"Who? Julie?"

I nodded and Dad sat back down on the bed. "Not now. She's trying to help you now. That's what's important."

"Do you want to though?"

"I don't know. We'll see. Is that what's wrong?"

"No."

"Then what is it?"

I scooted back down and curled onto my pillow. "I'm tired."

"I'll be back later," he said. He left and closed the door behind him. Sleep found me again easily.

*       *       *

I felt groggy when I woke up, but it was only nine o'clock. I climbed out of bed to use the bathroom, and when I finished Dad was standing at the top of the stairs waiting for me.

"Would you come downstairs for a little bit?" he asked.

I nodded and let him put his arm around my shoulder and lead me downstairs. When we got to the family room, Paul and Julie were sitting there, both looking concerned. My stomach and throat tightened. I felt trapped.

I curled up in a corner of the couch and rested my head on the arm. Dad sat in the recliner.

Julie shifted and leaned forward with her elbows on her knees. "Can you tell us what happened today?" she asked.

"I remembered," I said. They all reacted with surprise.

"You know who stabbed you?" Dad leaned forward.

I nodded. "It's one of Gretchen's friends. He doesn't go to our school, but I know him from when I was in the hospital last year. His name's Randy."

Dad raked his hand through his hair. "We have to call the police. We have to . . ."

"Dad, please, no. It's all going to be so horrible. It won't do any good anyway. I can't talk about this in some courtroom."

"You have to," Paul said. "You can't just let them get away with it."

"They already have. Nothing's going to make it any better for me."

"Beka, I know how hard this is. And if it involves Gretchen, I'm sure it's even harder. But they assaulted you. You'll regret it if you choose to do nothing."

"I won't. I promise."

"So you're just going to keep going to school with Gretchen, knowing she's capable of doing something like this?" Dad asked.

"But I don't know for sure." I straightened up then leaned my back on the couch.

We spent the next hour arguing back and forth. Everybody but me thought it was obvious what I should do. But all I wanted to do was forget about it. I ran my finger over the thin scar on my side. Now that I knew who it was, I could see his face so clearly in my mind, hear him whispering in my ear, feel him shove me to the ground. I could hear his breathing and . . . I squeezed my eyes shut to destroy the image.

I listened to them all and even agreed with what they were saying. But they weren't the ones who were going to have to keep recounting what happened, maybe in front of people, and Randy, in a courtroom. I didn't have the strength. I closed my eyes and shook my head.

"I know what you're saying, but I just can't do it. I can't."

Paul came over and sat next to me. "Beka, you're right. You can't." I looked over at him. "But God can. God can give you all the strength you need to face this."

For the first time since it happened, I felt my nose and eyes begin to burn. One tear, then another slipped down my cheek. "But why did He let it happen at all? You prayed I'd be safe." The sobs came from deep inside me and my shoulders shook. Paul wrapped his arms around me, and I let myself lean against him and cry, long and hard.

When there was nothing left in me, I looked up and used the tissues someone had pressed into my hand.

"I don't know why this happened. And we may never know why. But God is with you. And He did protect you.

Beka, you could have been killed out there." Dad's voice caught in his throat. "He's going to get you through this. You've got to believe that God has a purpose in all this."

I sniffed and wiped at my eyes. "A purpose?" My mind flew back to Dana's teaching on Sunday. She had said that God could take even the most horrible things in our lives and make something amazing out of them. She told a story about how a friend of hers had lost her baby son in a car accident. The woman had been devastated for a while but now, years later, she began a ministry that helped people all over the nation who had gone through the death of a child. Dana had said that even though losing the little boy was a terrible thing, a lot of good came out of it.

Could God really make something good out of this mess? Would He? I wanted to believe it, but my heart felt so weak.

"Can we pray for you?" Julie asked.

I nodded and dropped my chin to my chest. I let their words wash over me.

"Bring healing to her heart."

"Give her the strength she needs."

"Help her follow You."

"Make her clean."

Make her clean. That's what I wanted more than anything. I didn't want to feel dirty anymore. Make her clean. *God, make me clean. Help me follow You even when I don't understand You.*

By the time they were done, I felt a strange sense of peace. I still didn't want to go through with it, but I was ready to try. At least I wasn't alone. I looked around at the faces. Julie, Paul, and Dad had all been there when I needed them. They believed God would help me, and they were smart people. Maybe He would.

*　　*　　*

Before I went to sleep that night, I wrote in my journal.

*Find Me*

*On a dark road*
*In the quiet*
*I wonder if You're near*
*Are You close by?*
*On this dark road*
*I need to hear Your voice*

*Find me here*
*In the rainstorm*
*In the sunshine*
*In the darkness*
*Rescue me*
*From things I cannot see*
*Find me here*

*On my way home*
*I need to know*
*All that's in Your heart*
*On this rocky road*
*On my way home*
*Find my heart and make it Yours*

*Find me here*

Dad took me to the police station early in the morning and then dropped me off at school. The police hadn't been very encouraging. Since I didn't know his last name and they didn't have enough to pull medical files, they were going to have to talk to Gretchen about Randy. Why did I even care if Gretchen hated me? I shouldn't, but I did. Especially since the police told me that unless Randy gave up Gretchen, or they proved her involvement in some other way, then nothing would happen to her. That meant facing her my entire senior year.

Everywhere I went, teachers and kids smiled and waved at me. It was kind of bizarre. I had missed second period, so no Gretchen until seventh. Lori spent the entire lunch period trying to encourage me that I did the right thing.

"I just feel sick about the whole thing," I told her.

"I guess so. Look at everything you've been through and now this. That girl makes me so mad." Lori pounded her fist on the table.

I laughed. She looked like an angry little china doll. I was glad she had stuck with me.

"Let's talk about something else. What's up with Julie and your dad?"

"Dad says nothing right now. She's trying to help me and all. But I think he likes her."

"What about Gabby?"

I wrinkled my nose. "Anna rides with her twice a week, and she goes to our church. But she hasn't been around as much. I kind of feel bad because I was so angry with her, and they really were just friends."

"And Julie? What if they became more than friends?"

"I like her. But it still bothers me to think of my dad with someone else."

"Give it time I guess. That may change," Lori said.

I shrugged. "I just want summer to come so I don't have to deal with school for a while."

"And you've got your trip."

"No, I don't. They told us Sunday they're postponing it because of fighting in Port-au-Prince. They're hoping to go in the fall."

"The fall?" She tilted her head. "That means Josh won't be able to go."

"Exactly," I said. It was also why I wasn't sure I wanted to go either.

"Well, you'll see him Saturday. I can't wait to get all dressed up again." Lori wiped her mouth and stood up with her tray.

"I have to wear the same dress," I said.

"Oh, me too." She laughed. "But think about it. The guys will be wearing the same thing too."

We dumped our trays and waved good-bye. Only a few more classes left.

*     *     *

Gretchen never showed up for journalism. My mind raced. *Did the police come and get her? Does she know I told?* I chewed on the inside of my lip and tried to finish the proofreading that Ms. Adams had given me. I kept glancing over at Mai, who worked with a couple of other girls at the bank of computers, her features drawn tight in concentration. She would know where Gretchen was, but I didn't have the courage to ask her.

I read the same paragraph for the tenth time and pushed it away from me. Was there really anything I could do about it anyway? I would just have to wait and see. *Lord, please give me peace. Help me to trust You.*

I stood up and came face-to-face with Mai.

What did you do?" Mai asked.

"What?" I wanted to step away from her, but there was nowhere to go.

"Gretchen? Her parents came and got her today. What's going on?" Her face was hard.

"Why would that have anything to do with me?" If I sat back down, she'd be looking down at me.

"I know exactly what's going on. And I know you better make this all go away." Mai folded her arms and moved in even closer.

"I can't," I said. "I won't. I just told them the truth."

"The truth? The truth is worse things can happen."

"Is that a threat?" I asked.

"Oh." Mai put her finger to her chin and looked up. "And your sister's coming here next year. Isn't she? Hmmm. I'd hate for her to have to learn your lesson." She turned on her heel and walked back to the computers. I dropped back into my seat. Why couldn't all of this just go away?

*   *   *

I told Paul about Mai on the way home.

"She's all talk, Beka. Don't worry about her," Paul said.

"Easy for you to say. You won't even be here next year."

Paul frowned.

"I just wish I knew what was happening. It's torture not knowing."

"Do you want to go to the police station and ask? Would that make you feel better?"

I nodded and Paul drove right past our house to the police station. We asked for Detective Chalmers at the front desk and waited in a row of chairs. After a little bit he came out and led us to a small interview room.

"How can I help you today?" he asked. He shifted his weight back and forth while he stood by the door. He glanced at his watch and then smiled at me.

"Sorry. I know you're busy. I was just wondering what was going on with my case."

The detective flipped open the file he was holding and scanned it. Then he came back over and sat down.

"Well, we talked to Miss Stanley today. She admits to

knowing this Randy, but she said she was with him all night."

"She was at the beach party. Randy was down by the jetty attacking me. There were lots of people at the party. They'll tell you he wasn't there."

Detective Chalmers looked up and smiled. "It's still under investigation. We have several more interviews to conduct but . . ."

"It doesn't look good, does it?" I asked.

The detective pulled at his earlobe a couple of times and stretched his neck. "It's early yet. But unless Randy admits to Miss Stanley setting it up, we don't have a lot to go on. You never know though. Juvenile courts can be tough with cases like this, so she could still do detention time."

"And Randy?" Paul asked.

"That will be adult court, since he's eighteen. They need more evidence, but he could plead to a lesser charge. It's too early to tell. Give us a little more time."

He stood up and walked us back to the front of the police station.

"You hang in there now, okay?" Detective Chalmers patted me on the shoulder.

*     *     *

We got back in the car and I leaned back on the seat. "This is just awful," I said.

"He said it's not over. Let's just wait and see."

"But if Gretchen gets away with this, I think we

231

should just move. Or maybe boarding school. Do you think Dad would ask for a branch transfer?"

Paul laughed. "No, I don't. Don't give up yet. Let's see what God is going to do."

"Yeah, but what I want Him to do and what He actually does may be two different things."

"True." He nodded. "But either we believe He knows best or we don't."

I looked out the window as the trees flashed by. It was all so colorful and green. The ground and trees had woken up from winter in a riot of beauty, and here I still felt like winter inside. When would spring come to me?

*       *       *

The week dragged by. I was still getting lots of nice attention at school, when Gretchen and Mai weren't glaring at me. Gretchen was campaigning hard to be voted Junior Queen and was canvassing the school with her posters and pins. On Friday, Lori and I went to cast our votes before lunch and ran into Gretchen smiling and handing out Hershey's kisses in the foyer.

"Vote for me. Have you cast your vote for Junior Queen?" She smiled at a boy and a girl, shoving chocolates in their hands as they walked by. She turned to us smiling, but when she saw it was Lori and me, her smile fell from her face.

"I guess there's no point in asking for your vote," she said, looking at Lori.

Lori laughed. "I guess not."

Gretchen shifted her weight onto one hip, folded her

arms, and looked at me. "I always win. You remember that, Rebekah Madison."

"We'll just have to wait and see, now won't we?" I stepped forward to go toward the voting box, but Gretchen stepped in my path and squared her shoulders.

"I have the best lawyer money can buy. This will all be over before it even starts."

I pushed past her and went up to the little voting booth. Lori and I gave our names, and I scrawled Lori's name down on the paper and dropped it in the box.

"I can't believe her. I can't even tell you what I'd like to do to her," Lori said.

"Let's just go." I didn't want to think about Gretchen Stanley for one more minute.

*       *       *

When school was over, I wandered out to the baseball field. It was a beautiful day, but I felt down and didn't want to go home. I decided watching Paul's game would be a nice distraction. I climbed up the metal seats to the top row of bleachers and looked out on the field. Paul was throwing pitches to the catcher to warm up his arm. When he stopped to stretch, he looked up and caught my eye. He lifted his arm and waved. I waved back and settled against the bars behind me.

The game started, and I watched my brother strike out the first three batters from the other team. They came in to bat, and I dug out my trig homework. Baseball games were long, and I might as well get something done. I didn't want to have any homework tomorrow. I had to take Anna out to Gabby's for her lesson, and then I could go to Lori's to get ready for the prom. My mind drifted to Josh. I wondered what it would be like if he weren't leaving.

"Beka."

I looked over to see Mark standing next to the bleachers looking up at me. We stayed that way for several minutes, neither of us speaking. I wasn't even sure what to say. He hadn't talked to me since the attack, and I had only seen glimpses of him at school. It was like he was avoiding me.

He broke eye contact and walked around to the front of the bleachers, climbing and moving up the seats around several groups of people in front of me. He sat in front of me and leaned his elbows on his knees.

"I owe you an apology," he said.

"Mark, you . . ." I started, but he held up his hand.

"Let me say this. Please? I was angry with you. So angry. I put myself out there and you rejected me."

I fought the urge to respond.

"But I realized that you were right. I went to youth group last night and, well, it wasn't anything they said, I just realized how far away from God I was. I was over here and God was way over there." He pointed out toward the athletic fields. "I've got some things to get right. When we were together, well, it made me want to do things we shouldn't. I never thought I was pushing you. But I was. The whole time. You were right to put a stop to it."

"Mark."

"I'm sorry. And I'm sorry for blowing you off after

what happened to you. I hated that anybody hurt you. I'm so sorry."

"I understand." I gave him a small smile. "I'm glad you told me though. It helps."

"I should have stopped by or called. But I was so mad."

"You mentioned that," I said.

He smiled at me. "I'm not angry anymore. I feel like an idiot. And it's going to take me some time to get things straightened out with God. I was trying to get along with my parents and follow their rules and all, but God," he shook his head, "I guess I didn't want anything to do with Him."

"You told me you believed."

"I do believe. But I didn't want somebody else telling me what to do. After seeing how I hurt you, maybe I need more help than I think."

"It's confusing stuff, isn't it? This God business."

He held his hand on his chest. "Way down inside, I just know I have to stop messing around. I've got to settle this."

"Settle what?"

"Who's in charge. And it's gonna take some time probably to earn your dad's trust. And yours." He looked in my eyes and smiled. "I'm gonna win back your heart, Beka Madison."

I felt myself blush. And almost immediately I had a sinking feeling. "I have another date for prom. Dad wasn't going to let me go with you and . . ."

"I figured you did. I don't mind." He lifted his eyebrows. "Just promise you won't fall in love with him."

Mark stood up and moved over next to me on the top bleacher. He watched my brother wind up and let a pitch fly across the plate. The batter never had a chance.

He wanted to win my heart. The words felt soft and warm in my thoughts. But as I rolled them over in my mind, something shifted. *I want to win your heart first.* The words came from deep inside, and even though they sounded like my thoughts, I knew in an instant God had spoken. Didn't God have my heart? I thought about it. My heart seemed to fly in all different directions. *How do you learn to love God? How do you know what love looks like?* The questions filled my mind.

I sat next to Mark, both of us looking toward the game, but I wasn't watching. God wanted to win my heart. What an amazing thought.

I knocked on Lori's door right at one o'clock. I was excited and a little nervous to go out with Josh again. I didn't know exactly what he thought of me. He wanted to write to me, but he had never told me how he felt about me or anything. I just didn't know what to make of it.

Lori opened the door dressed in a robe with a towel on top of her head. She pulled me inside.

"Brian will love that outfit," I teased.

"Ya think?" She curtsied. "Come on, Mom's got something in her room, and she said she won't show me until you get here."

Megan came around the corner wiping her hands on

a dish towel. We both turned toward her. "Now, I know I shouldn't have." She walked up the stairs, and we followed her. She put her hand on the doorknob to her room and smiled. "I just couldn't resist. Now, they're secondhand but they're in really good shape. Who wants to wear the same thing twice?"

She opened the door, and lying out on the bed were six formal dresses.

"Wow."

We both walked over and looked at them. Lori picked up a purple and black one. "There are only two of us, Mom."

"I know, but I wasn't sure which ones you'd like and I tell you, women at sales racks can be vicious. I had to move fast." She made a Ninja move with her arms.

Lori and I laughed. "Well, I'm trying on this one." Lori stepped inside the bathroom.

"See anything you like?" Megan asked.

"Yes, they're all pretty. I like this green one, but my other dress was green. Maybe this blue one." I lifted up a silky periwinkle dress with a sheer half-layer over the back of the skirt.

"Try it," she said.

Lori and I both loved the new dresses, and Megan took off with the colors and our shoe sizes to find matching shoes while Lori and I started getting ready.

"I'm so excited. Every time I see Brian I just turn to mush."

"So you're still feeling the same about him?" I asked.

"Totally." Lori pulled a comb through her wet hair, and I looked down at my own.

"Does this still smell like farm to you?" I held out a section of my hair, and Lori sniffed it.

"It smells like strawberries. Did you go out to Gabby's today?"

"Yeah. And you'd be proud of me. I apologized for putting her in that position when she caught me with Mark." I brushed my hair while Lori started on her nails.

"So you talked to her?"

"Just a little bit after Anna's lesson. She asked me about my birthday. You know, her brother lives out in LA, and he used to be a musician. She told me when I told her about my guitar."

"That's really cool. He's not one anymore?"

"He doesn't play anymore, I guess, but he does something out there."

"So everything's cool with her?"

"Pretty much. She reminded me that I didn't have anything to worry about with her and my dad, but when she said it, her eyes looked sad. Even Anna noticed."

"She must have liked your dad more than your dad liked her."

"I suppose." I almost felt sorry for her.

\*     \*     \*

After a bit Megan came back with shoes that fit perfectly. She hurried to get our hair curled and put up while we finished our makeup. We were ready with ten minutes to spare. We waited in the living room, and the doorbell rang right at five. Josh looked amazing, and his smile made my toes curl.

Megan began her picture-taking frenzy, moving us all around in different positions. Kari Lynn wanted her picture taken with us again, and Lori's dad leaned on the dining room wall watching it all. When Megan finally finished, the boys led us outside to a long white limo and took us to a restaurant called The Log Cabin, just outside of town. It was really expensive, so Lori and I whispered behind the menus so we would both order something close to the same price.

Dinner was wonderful, and during the limo ride to The Plaza, Josh laid his hand on top of mine. I wasn't sure whether to curl my fingers around his or just stay in that position. We were there before I had figured out what to do, and we were climbing out in front of the hotel.

The prom theme was "Hollywood Premiere," so as soon as we stepped out of the limo, we were greeted with a real red carpet and dozens of flashes from photographers lined up behind velvet ropes. I grinned. It made me feel like a star. Lori and I took Brian's and Josh's arms, and they led us down the carpet into the grand entrance foyer of The Plaza. We followed the signs back to the ballroom and gave our tickets to the sophomores at the door. The inside was decked out with velvet ropes, movie posters in fake gold frames, Oscar statues, and fabric draped from the ceilings in designs. I could tell that Gretchen was the chairman of the Junior Prom committee. Only Gretchen would turn the prom into the Academy Awards.

I saw Gretchen and Jeremy standing by the punch table almost as soon as we walked in. She was wearing a formfitting black and red dress with a slit practically up to her hip. She looked over and saw the group of us but made no reaction. She said something to Jeremy and then started walking our way. I squeezed Josh's arm.

"What's wrong?" he asked.

"That's Gretchen. Coming toward us." I took a deep breath.

"Well," she said stopping in front of us, "I haven't seen you around here before." She looked Josh up and down to the point that it even embarrassed me. "Are you a cousin or something?" she asked.

Josh pulled me closer. "Not even close."

Gretchen raised her eyebrows and walked past me whispering, "I'm surprised you even bothered to come."

Josh laced his fingers through mine. "Never mind about her. You're all mine tonight."

Josh and I moved into the room and found a table to sit at, marking the cards to reserve our spot. Lori and Brian were already on the dance floor. Paul and his date, Tiffany, came by and said hi briefly on their way to the dance floor.

"I'm sorry about that," I said to Josh.

"You have nothing to be sorry about," he said. "I'm glad you let me bring you. Come on. Why don't we go dance?"

I smiled and let him lead me out on the dance floor. It was a slow song, so he put his hands on my waist and moved me in a slow circle. The music surrounded us, and it felt just about perfect. For a while it was really nice. The music was good and easy to dance to. I loved talking with Josh and feeling him close. It didn't hurt that I knew Gretchen and Mai were probably watching us too.

But things started changing after the first hour. The music started getting louder, and it seemed like all the people on the dance floor were dancing in these small huddles. When Josh and I got pulled into one, we saw a girl in the middle dancing suggestively in front of each person in the circle. Josh grabbed my hand and we hurried back to our table. I was glad not to see any more.

"I'm sorry," I said to him. "I didn't realize."

"Stop apologizing. It's not your fault."

We sat there for a few minutes. It felt awkward, like the evening had been spoiled somehow. Lori and Brian arrived a few minutes later.

"Do you know what they're doing in there?" Lori pointed to the dance floor.

I nodded. "Josh and I got an up close look, unfortunately."

"It's awful. I mean this one girl was . . . eeeewww." She put her hand over her eyes and shook her head.

"Maybe we should go," I said. I looked out on the dance floor where sexually charged teenagers had replaced the fun and easy dances. It just felt all wrong.

"We can't go yet. Let's at least wait to hear the Junior Queen announcement," Lori said.

"Why do I want to stay to see Gretchen get a crown?"

"She may not win. Let's just stay and find out, then we can go."

I looked at Josh, and he shrugged one shoulder and sat back in his chair. Paul and Tiffany came and sat down with us, telling us their version of the dancing going on and agreeing with us that we'd go really soon. I really liked Tiffany, and I could tell she liked Paul. She kept watching him and laughed every time he made a joke. We talked and had snacks and punch until the band stopped playing, and Gretchen walked onto the stage carrying a crown and a big bouquet of flowers. She must have been wearing a wireless mike, because her voice echoed through the room.

"I'd like to welcome you all to the Junior-Senior Prom!" she said. Everyone applauded, and when they stopped she continued. "As the Prom Committee Chairperson, I have the honor of announcing this year's Junior Queen." She handed the bouquet and crown to a girl standing next to her on stage and took an envelope from the principal, Mrs. Brynwit.

"Now, the results are all counted and checked by Mr. Yard in the math department, so no one but them knows what's in this envelope." You could hear her ripping open the envelope by her microphone. "And your Junior Queen is . . ." She stopped and looked up for a moment, then looked back down at the paper. Her excited voice became flat. "Your Junior Queen is Rebekah Madison."

The crowd broke into applause, and I looked at everybody at the table. They were all smiling and clapping.

"That can't be," I said.

Lori grinned. "Go. Gretchen's waiting to crown you."

Josh leaned over and hugged me with a big grin on his face.

I got up, unsure my knees would hold me, and made my way up onto the stage. Gretchen didn't smile, and her eyes flashed. She shoved the bouquet in my hand and dropped the small tiara on top of my head. I looked out at everyone and tried to smile. I could hardly believe it. I could feel Gretchen's anger seeping out of her as she stood next to me.

"Okay. That's enough guys, we still have to do your Senior Queen." Gretchen glared at me. "Congratulations Beka." She jutted her chin toward the stairs, and I climbed down them and went out the door into the foyer. I needed a moment to think. I sat down on one of the cushy benches outside the restrooms to catch my breath. I heard the applause and the announcement of the Senior Queen and then Gretchen thanking everybody for coming and telling them to have a great time. While the applause was still going on, I saw a flash of black and red come through the doors.

I stood up quickly as Gretchen strode toward me, her dress flapping and her eyes dark.

"Just who do you think you are?" she said. "That's my crown."

I felt calm. "Apparently not this time," I said.

"You're going to pay for this, I swear. And next time I'll find someone who's not an idiot like Randy. You'll regret crossing me, Madison. You won't get off this easy."

"You don't scare me, Gretchen. Not anymore." I hoped the words would become true as I said them out loud.

The door behind Gretchen flew open. Mai came running out and tore something off of Gretchen and clutched it in the folds of her dress. I couldn't see what it was.

"What are you doing?" Gretchen demanded.

Mai leaned in and whispered in Gretchen's ear. Gretchen swore, and she and Mai tore off down the hallway. Mrs. Brynwit and a couple of other teachers threw open the doors and looked around.

"Where did Miss Stanley go?" Mrs. Brynwit asked.

I pointed down the hallway, and the four of them followed after her.

What was going on?

Lori, Josh, and Paul were the next to come through the door.

"I can't believe that," Lori said.

"I know. I never thought anybody would vote for me," I said.

"No," Paul said. "Gretchen was wearing her mike. The whole room just heard her threaten you and confess to setting you up."

"What?"

"We all heard what she said to you. She was still wearing the mike," Lori repeated.

I dropped back onto the bench stunned.

"And you were awesome, by the way," Josh said.

I looked up at him and then around at Paul and Lori.

"Let's go back in," Lori said. "Just for a few minutes." Josh offered his arm, and right before we walked through the door, he leaned down and kissed me quickly on the cheek. I don't think my feet even touched the ground on the way in. When we stepped into the ballroom, the whole room broke into applause and the people sitting down stood up. I was overwhelmed. They applauded for what seemed like forever.

When the applause finally died down, the lead guitarist of the band came to the mike. "I'm not sure what happened here tonight. But it's time to bring this party up."

They played a loud song, and the six of us decided to go back to Paul's and my house to spend the rest of the evening. I didn't see Gretchen or Mai anywhere on our way out. And it didn't matter to me what might be happening. Because whatever it was, Gretchen brought it on herself this time.

*　　　*　　　*

We stopped by the video store and Josh passed around his cell phone so Tiffany and Lori and Brian could call home and let their parents know where they were. When we got home, Dad sat and listened as we told him the events of the evening, and then we played Taboo, watched movies, and ate popcorn late into the night. It was a night I knew I would remember for a long time.

I stood with Lucy, Anna, and my dad as the senior class marched into the football stadium. Josh sat behind us with a couple of Paul's friends from church, and Lori and Megan came as well. Then there were my mom's parents and my dad's brother and his family sitting a few seats to our right. I looked for Paul's face in the sea of red and white gowns and spotted him toward the middle of the group. This was it. Paul's graduation brought an end to a chapter in our lives. He would still be home for the summer, but my world was shifting and I could see the signs of it everywhere.

The prom had made things different at school. I felt included when I was there, and for the first time in my life, felt really comfortable being there. I knew things could change again, but the year had finished out, and I had a whole summer stretching ahead to relax and enjoy.

The police arrested and charged Gretchen the night of prom with conspiracy to commit a felony. She pointed the finger at Randy and he pointed one at her, and they both ended up charged. I never even had to go to court because they ended up pleading guilty. The judge sentenced her to twelve months in detention with ten months suspended. It basically meant that she would spend the summer in detention, but wouldn't have to serve the rest unless she got in trouble again. Randy got three years, but he was going to jail because he was an adult. The other two got intensive probation. It all happened so fast, I hardly had time to digest it all.

Paul had graduated at the top of his class, but he had missed valedictorian by just a few points. We listened to the speech and then watched as the names were called one by one. When they said Paul's name, we all stood up and clapped and waved. I snapped pictures of him accepting his diploma and shaking hands with the principal and vice principal. My throat tightened. I wasn't ready to say good-bye.

He waved as he walked down the sidelines and then circled back to his seat as they continued calling out the names. When it was all over, Paul hurried over to us, and I asked Megan if she would take a couple of pictures of all of us. Paul stood in the center and Dad stood next to him. Lucy, Anna, and I huddled in, and we all smiled as Megan snapped away.

It was our first family picture without Mom.

My eyes burned, but I pinched the bridge of my nose to keep from crying.

"Are you alright?" Josh asked.

I smiled. "I'm gonna miss him, that's all."

Josh nodded and we both watched him spin Anna around in a circle, Paul's red robe flying out behind him. "Just try to enjoy the summer. That's what I plan to do." Josh looked at me and smiled.

I smiled back. It was going to be a busy couple of months. I had accepted the job at Megan's studio and had arranged to take two guitar lessons a week during the summer. And of course, there was Josh. He had made several comments over the last couple of weeks about getting together this summer. I wasn't totally sure what he meant, but I was anxious to find out. I wasn't planning on approaching the Mark topic with Dad anytime soon, so I focused my thoughts on Josh, wondering if it was a mistake since he would be leaving in the middle of August. But I couldn't change it, so I might as well just sit back and enjoy the ride.

*     *     *

Paul asked Dad to swing by the cemetery on our way back to the house, where relatives and friends were waiting to congratulate Paul. We all climbed out of the car, but we let Paul go on ahead of us. He walked the short distance and stood at the foot of Mom's grave, still wearing his robe. A few minutes later he fell to his knees, and we watched as his shoulders hunched for several minutes. Then he stood back up and walked up to the headstone. He walked back to us, and when he did I could see his red cap sitting on the top of the gravestone.

When he got back to us, his face was red and his eyes were wet. Dad grabbed him in a hug, and then Anna and Lucy and I wrapped our arms around them both and each other. We stood there for a long time holding one another.

After a while, we climbed back in the car, and Dad drove us home to the house full of people who would never really understand what we had been through together. Part of me wanted to tell Dad to keep driving and take us to a quiet lunch together. But he pulled into our driveway where the cars were already lined up.

We looked around at each other for several minutes before climbing out of the car and going inside. As we climbed the stairs, Paul put his arm around my shoulder and squeezed. He didn't have to say a thing.

## Visit
## www.becomingbeka.com

- ❑ Fun Quizzes
- ❑ Contests
- ❑ Free Bookmarks
- ❑ Ask Questions
- ❑ Get Answers

I hope you'll visit me online. Thanks for reading!

*Sarah*

### Book #1 of the Becoming Beka series

ISBN: 0-8024-6451-3

EAN/ISBN-13: 978-0-8024-6451-4

Beka has been trying to move on with her life since her mother's tragic accident, but it feels like she's going nowhere fast.

Things are not so good at home. Beka's brother and sisters won't leave her alone. Her scary dreams keep coming back. And worst of all, Beka has a secret she can't share with anyone, especially not her family.

As it turns out, Beka's not the only person with secrets. But before she can get a new start on life, she'll have to be honest about who she is.

*Book #2 of the Becoming Beka series*

ISBN: 0-8024-6452-1

EAN/ISBN-13: 978-0-8024-6452-1

When Beka heads back to school with a newfound faith, she expects some special feeling, some enlightenment, something different. But what she feels is . . . nothing. In fact, what she faces is a series of tough choices.

For some reason Gretchen, the most powerful and popular girl in school, takes an interest in Beka, and Beka finds herself enjoying the popularity. But Gretchen's attention comes with a price. Her fascination with the occult threatens to lure Beka into the dark web of tarot cards, crystals and spells.

Then there's Mark, who wants to spend time with Beka behind her father's back. And the youth group her father wants her to join. And the tension of winning back her siblings' and her father's trust. Not to mention her studies.

It adds up to pressure and confusion Beka may be ill-equipped to handle.

Since 1894, Moody Publishers has been dedicated to equip and motivate people to advance the cause of Christ by publishing evangelical Christian literature and other media for all ages, around the world. Because we are a ministry of the Moody Bible Institute of Chicago, a portion of the proceeds from the sale of this book go to train the next generation of Christian leaders.

If we may serve you in any way in your spiritual journey toward understanding Christ and the Christian life, please contact us at www.moodypublishers.com.

*"All Scripture is God-breathed and is useful for teaching, rebuking, correcting and training in righteousness, so that the man of God may be thoroughly equipped for every good work."*
—2 TIMOTHY 3:16, 17

MOODY
PUBLISHERS

THE NAME YOU CAN TRUST®

## THE PASSAGE TEAM

**ACQUIRING EDITOR**
Andy McGuire

**BACK COVER COPY**
Lisa Ann Cockrel

**COPY EDITOR**
Cheryl Dunlop

**COVER DESIGN**
LeVan Fisher Design

**COVER PHOTO**
Haruka Demura/Photonica

**INTERIOR DESIGN**
Ragont Design

**PRINTING AND BINDING**
Bethany Press International

*The typeface for the text of this book is*
***Aetna JY***